by

Bethany Maines
&
Juel Lugo

 Blue Zephyr Press
2661 N. Pearl, #360
Tacoma WA 98407

Cover art by **LILT**.

ISBN-13: 979-8-9867745-5-8

Dedication

While Covid kept everyone inside, Juel Lugo and Bethany Maines may have overdosed on one too many romantic comedies. So much so that they decided to write their own tale of romance. And with all the confidence that a decade of collaboration on other creative projects could give them, they did just that. Having produced a novel and an award-winning script, they feel successful in their joint venture and hope you enjoy this sun soaked, wine-tinged romance. It is dedicated to all the other rom-com movie fans out there.

Table of Contents

PART 1:

The Italian...
Red Wine

We suggest savoring this section with a glass of Nebbiolo – a rare gem from Washington that beckons the adventurous heart. The search for it becomes a journey of its own, making each sip that much sweeter. Nebbiolo is America's love letter to Barolo, a passion only truly named in the hills of Italy.

Our pick the *2020 Nebbiolo from Saviah Cellars.*

TASTING NOTES: Silky tannins and rich, bright flavors of ripe cherry, wild strawberry, and red raspberries. The finish is silky, long, and generous. This particular Nebbiolo was made lovingly with it's cap was punched down two to three times per day by hand until the wine completed primary fermentation.

CHAPTER 1
A Penny's Worth

Simone

Simone Laurent nursed her vintage silver and turquoise motorhome off the freeway and prayed it all the way up to the sign that read: LUCKLESS, WA, 1 MILE. There, it died with an unhappy belch of smoke.

"No, Matilda, no. Just a little further. We're almost there!"

With a futile hope, she twisted the key off and on. The motor made a grinding, unhappy noise, and Simone flopped forward over the steering wheel.

Beside her, a wire-haired terrier made a circle in the passenger seat and let out a small yip of distress.

"I don't believe in luck," said Simone, raising her head with a sniff. "This is not a bad sign. There is nothing unlucky going on." She wiped her nose and looked at the dog. "Just because this is the final stop to take Dad's ashes and Matilda chooses now to conk out does not mean we're luckless."

Skipper gave a little doggy sneeze and shifted in his seat.

"It just means," Simone straightened her spine and tried to put on a brave face. "that when the going gets tough, the tough have to get…" Her bottom lip wobbled. "Going." Skipper jumped from his seat into hers and began to lick her face.

"No, we got this. We totally got this," she said, hugging Skipper. "We *are* tough. After all, we've made it through forty-nine other states, and we're not going to let this one slow us down just because it's the last state, our home died, and it's the one stop that really matters. I'm sure Matilda's not dead. She's just…" Skipper cocked his head to one side, waiting. "Taking a little nap. We will persevere, and we will triumph."

Skipper wagged his tail and looked like he completely believed her. Which was good because Simone wasn't sure she believed it herself.

"Besides, it's not like anyone is coming to rescue us. We're on our own, Skipper. And we really can do it. Because we are Laurents, and Laurents can do anything."

Simone was well-aware that if her dog was the Skipper, that meant, in the greater pantheon of *Gilligan's Island*, that she was the Little Buddy. However, the dog had come to her on a very dark, icy night in the middle of South Dakota, wearing nothing but a bandana with SKIPPER emblazoned on it. Questioning of houses in the vicinity had uncovered the fact that someone had been seen dumping Skipper out of their car a few days earlier. So, realizing that he had lost everything else, Simone was reluctant to also take his name. Besides, there were days when she felt every bit as competent as Gilligan. Today was starting to feel like a Gilligan day.

Simone pulled out her phone to locate a garage and a tow truck that she no doubt would regret paying for and realized she had no bars. So far Luckless Washington was living up to its name.

"I think we're walking, Skipper," she said to the dog. He sneezed again. "Yeah," she agreed. That's how I feel about it."

Reluctantly, Simone gathered her dark hair into a ponytail, put the leash on the dog, and slung her camera bag slash purse across her body. Then, locking the doors to the only home she had left, Simone set out for the town of Luckless.

Jordan

Jordan Ryan pushed his vintage 1964 Alfa Romeo Spider convertible into the lot of Ryan's garage. His sister Michelle, dressed in blue work overalls, paused, one foot up on the running board of the Ryan's Garage tow truck.

"Oh, man, not again!" Michelle shook her head, and her brown ponytail shoved out the back of her red trucker cap, bounced back and forth in counterpoint.

Jordan paused and leaned against his car, sweating through his t-shirt and panting.

"Yeah, again. I swear to God I'm going to sell this pile of junk."

"Whatever, baby brother. You know that come tomorrow, you'll be in church praying to the big man to help you fix it," said Michelle with a laugh.

"I need to give it up," said Jordan. "There's no point."

"Whiner," said Michelle, with the kind of sympathy that only an older sister could get away with. "Did you even make it out of town?"

"Barely," said Jordan. "I stopped into the office for a few minutes and then hit the road. Or at least I tried to. I think I hit the road a little too hard."

Michelle paused as if reviewing his sentence. "What'd you go to the office for? Didn't you say it was your day off?" Michelle raised her eyebrows, and Jordan ignored the hint of a *tone*. She was going into mom-mode. "First Saturday off in three months or something? You had some sort of rhapsody about pancakes and the open road."

"That's what it was supposed to be," said Jordan with an exasperated groan. "First Saturday off in three months. It's the crush. You know how it is. All hands on deck when the grapes come in. I just snuck in to get a few things in order for Monday. No one even knew I was there. Everything was fine until I got to the fountain."

"Sorry," said Michelle, but chuckling, which was no kind of sympathy at all. "The lesson there is that you shouldn't have stopped at the office on your day off. You pissed off the car gods."

"Thanks so much. You're the best sister ever," said Jordan sarcastically. "Can we not have this discussion right now?"

"OK, how about: that's what you get for buying Italian," said Michelle, with a grin, and Jordan rolled his eyes. "Anyway," continued Michelle. "I've got to go pull a cow out of a hole, but I can help you look at it when I get back."

"You need a tow truck to pull a cow out of a hole?" asked Jordan, raising his eyebrows over his aviators.

"It's Gordon Beauford's prize Highland Heifer."

"Those things are about as cute as a cow can be, but that particular one is dumber than a brick. Didn't it get stuck in a hedge a couple of months ago?" asked Jordan, eyeing the distance from his car to the garage lift and trying to work up the energy for the final push.

"Yup. And now it's stuck in a hole. Easy money as far as I'm concerned. You want me to help you push her onto the lift?"

Jordan sighed and hung his head. "Yes, please."

"You take the back," she said, shooing him away from the driver's side. "It's better if I do the steering."

"You're the boss," said Jordan, doing as he was told. Michelle had inherited the business from their father. While Jordan had spent summers helping out in the garage growing up and enjoyed tinkering with his antique pile of junk, it was Michelle who knew the ins and outs of every car in a fifty-mile radius. When it came to the confines of Ryan's Garage, Michelle was *the* Ryan in charge.

Between them, they got the convertible secured and up on the lift.

"OK," said Michelle, giving the little car a friendly pat. "I'll be back in a bit. Don't get carried away and decide to rebuild the manifold or something while I'm gone. I need the lift if nothing else."

"I won't," said Jordan. "I'm pretty sure it was a radiator hose. I think I just need to get her open and do a replacement."

"I've got those in stock. I'll be back in a bit. Stewie is off today, so do me a favor and answer the phone if it rings. I'll probably be back in a couple of hours."

"Will do," said Jordan.

Michelle waved as she left, and Jordan waved back.

"Why, baby?" he asked the car when she was gone. "You couldn't keep it together for one cruise out to Spokane and back?"

With a sigh, he stripped out of his sweaty t-shirt, hung it by the fan, and then went to find the needed tools.

Simone

Simone and Skipper trudged along the road. It was so hot that Simone could see illusions of water rippling on the asphalt in front of them. The sun stabbed down at them, angry at their impertinent efforts to travel abroad during the heat of the day. Simone made Skipper walk in the stick-dry grass on the verge of the road so he wouldn't burn his paws on the pavement, but his little tongue was hanging out. The land around them was parched and dusty brown except on the hill away to her left, where a beautiful white building crouched among a field of lush greenery. The sunlight looked softer over there as if the owner had made the appropriate sacrifices, and the fiery orb above them looked kindly upon the entire place.

"Must be nice," said Simone to Skipper with a sigh. Lately, she had found herself envying buildings. When she first started her journey, she had been elated to leave the dust of Colorado behind her. She'd been tied to the place for so long through love and grief and endless monotonous round trips between home and hospice care that when the time came, she had left without a second thought. But a year later, her journey was nearly done and she was tired of sleeping in the tiny berth of the motorhome and wished she could remember what it felt like to water a garden or watch the sunset from a porch.

"You know, Skipper," said Simone, trying not to pant like the dog. "When I promised Dad I would take his ashes to all fifty states, I really thought somehow that there would be less walking. Or at least less sweating. Why did he have to be born here anyway? Couldn't he have been born somewhere nice? Like… Maine. Maine was nice. Or just the other half of this stupid state. Do you know they have trees on the other side of those mountains?"

She flapped her hand in the general direction of the Cascade mountain range, painted blue and purple by distance.

"But no… He had to go and be born in Luckless Washington. What kind of stupid name is that, anyway? Why couldn't they name it something like *The Lucky Place Where Simone Will Win the Lottery*? That would be an excellent name."

Simone glanced at Skipper, who gave her a very doggy-type look.

"Yeah, I know. Not very likely. But it would be nice because I have to tell you, bud, we are almost out of cash. I will have to find a job as soon as we make it back to Colorado. Otherwise, we're *both* going to be eating dog food. I really shouldn't have splurged for the trip to Hawaii, but I promised Dad all fifty states, and I wasn't going to miss it by one."

Simone wiped her face as they crested a hill and paused, staring down at a vision of the promised land. The town of Luckless could be seen through the haze of heat, but at the foot of the hill was a beautiful marble fountain throwing glimmering arcs of water into the air in sprightly defiance of the heat. It was surrounded by an oasis of blooming flowers and framed by a pair of maples waving gently and flashing the silver undersides of their leaves like schools of fish swimming in the turquoise sky and turning in the current of the breeze.

"Oh," breathed Simone in awe, reaching for her camera. They hurried down the gentle slope of the hill, and when they reached the fountain, Skipper bounded over the edge and plunged into the pool. Simone approached more slowly, noting the signpost indicating Luckless was a quarter-mile ahead while the Amante Winery was the next left. Skipper stood in the fountain, the water up to his shoulders, lapping at the waterfall that poured from the jug of a winged and gleeful cherub, while above him, a more stately Cupid with his bow drawn posed thoughtfully as if picking out his target.

Simone scooped some water and splashed it over her neck, letting it trickle down into her cleavage and in a little rivulet down her spine.

"Skipper, come out of there. I want to take a picture."

Skipper was used to this command and did as he was told, but slowly, flicking his tongue into the water as he went. He hopped down and went to investigate the landscaping for exciting smells. Skipper knew better than to go into a road, and there weren't any cars anyway, so she let him drag his leash along after him and focused on the fountain. It looked old and crafted in an Italian style with all the gorgeous attention to detail that only came from a master carver. It was as though the heavens had parted and dropped a massive chunk of Italy into the middle of Eastern Washington.

Simone lined up her shot and snapped a few, then paused to add a filter to her lens. She adjusted her position and then re-framed and snapped another dozen photos. She squinted at her camera, using her hand to shade the tiny screen, trying to see the results, but the glare was too high.

"Get anything good?" asked a friendly voice, and Simone looked up in surprise. A man crossed the road, approaching the fountain. He looked to be in his sixties, with white hair, and had a tall walking stick in one hand, wore a white collared shirt, dark trousers, tall boots, and a wide-brimmed straw sun hat. Like the fountain, he looked as if he was visiting from Italy.

"I don't know," said Simone. "It's really the wrong time of day. High sun is always harsh, but it's so beautiful, I had to try."

Skipper came over to snuffle the man's boots.

"Well, hello, little friend," said the man, bending down to pat Skipper's head.

"That's Skipper," said Simone.

"Pleased to meet you, Skipper. I'm Mateo."

"I'm Simone. I actually can't even see the photos I did take," she complained, frowning at her camera. "It's too bright."

Mateo laughed. "Unfortunate. Perhaps we could use my hat as a shade?" he suggested, taking it off and holding it out. Simone came over, and he shaded the camera, peering over her shoulder to see the pictures. Simone felt a little silly showing her photos to a man she'd just met but realized it wasn't any different than load-ing them to Instagram, so she hit the recall button and flipped through the photos.

"Hmm," said Simone, not liking her early efforts and finally settling on one that she thought might be worth the time of downloading. "That one isn't bad."

Mateo laughed. "Those are all beautiful. You are too critical. I would hang up any of those."

Simone smiled. "Thanks. But the subject matter makes it easy. The fountain is amazing. It wasn't something I expected to see here. Do you know where it came from?"

"From the Amante Estate in Italy," said Mateo.

"Amante like the winery?" asked Simone, pointing at the road sign.

"The very same," he said. "The Amante family sided with the Allies and made the mistake of voicing a few opinions that were... unpopular—shall we say?—with Mussolini, and he burned the estate to the ground. The surviving family members fled Italy and ended up here. After the war, they brought over the only thing that remained of their family villa—this fountain. Unfortunately, Lorenzo, six horses, and a truck still could not get it up the hill to the winery. So here it sits. After some time, Lorenzo gifted it to the town, and now it welcomes visitors. It is said that if you toss a coin in the fountain as a gift to Cupid, you will meet your true love. I like to come by on my walk and do a little weeding."

"That's a delightful story," said Simone. "Well, not the part about Mussolini. But the part about finding true love. And it was certainly a wonderful welcome for Skipper and me. My motorhome broke down a little ways back, and I have no cell service."

"Oh, no! Are you all right?" Mateo looked genuinely concerned.

"We're fine. Just hot. And I'm hoping there is a garage somewhere close or better phone service in town."

"Yes, and yes," said Mateo. "Ryan's Garage is straight ahead on this road. They're just a few blocks into town and will be able to help you. And the service seems to pick up the second you cross First Street. Most annoying, but better than it used to be."

"Oh, that's fantastic!" said Simone, feeling relieved. "I'm so glad I met you." Simone reached down and picked up Skipper's leash. "Come on, Skipper. Let's go find someone to rescue our house."

Mateo laughed. "But wait," he said as she stepped toward the road. "Have you made your offering?" He gestured to Cupid, and Simone laughed.

"I'm not sure love is in the cards for me," she said.

Mateo fished in his pocket and pulled out a coin. "Nonsense! It is never too late for love." He held out the penny to Simone.

"Well," she said, taking the coin after a moment's hesitation, "I suppose it couldn't hurt." She turned to face the fountain. "Cupid, a penny's worth of love, please." She kissed the coin and tossed it into the bubbling water at Cupid's feet.

"It's not the amount that matters," said Mateo. "It's the gift itself."

Simone laughed. "We'll see. Thanks for the directions and the penny!"

"Of course! Good luck!"

Simone left Mateo with a wave and headed into town feeling lighter than she had a few minutes earlier.

Jordan

Jordan sucked his finger where he'd pinched it and stared in exasperation at the tiny space that he was expected to wedge his hand and a wrench into. Had all mechanics in 1964 been tiny, dainty people with fingers the size of a china doll's? The fan was making a racket, but barely making a breeze, but at least it was competing with the radio that was playing nothing but eighties throw-back hits. He'd never heard this particular song before, but it had an annoying bell-ringing effect.

Maybe if he lowered the lift a little and wedged his hand in from the left, he could—

A cold, wet thing pressed against his elbow as he leaned on the edge of the pit, and Jordan yelled and jerked away from the unexpected sensation, knocking an entire tray of socket wrenches onto the floor with a clatter. He made a grab for them as they went but only managed to crack his head against the lift mechanism.

"Are you OK?" asked a concerned female voice.

Jordan gingerly stood up and stared into a pair of gorgeous hazel eyes with miles of dark lashes. She looked about twenty-five and had near-black hair pulled back into a ponytail away from a delicate oval face and a skeptical expression. Jordan scanned the rest of her—from the camera dangling around her neck, the sensible walking shoes, and the dog sitting at her feet and realized two things. While drop-dead pretty was his preferred type of girl, she fell under the heading of his least favorite kind of human being: tourist. The dog even had a bandana with his name on it.

"No, I'm not OK!" he snapped, rubbing his head, realizing too late that when he'd hit his head, he'd picked up grease from the lift jack and had just smeared it through his hair. "You aren't supposed to be back here, and neither is your dog!"

The dog, who had been in the midst of a vigorous ear scratch, paused, leg still in the air, looking shocked.

"Well, I've been ringing the bell for the last three minutes," she said icily. "Was there another way I was supposed to get your attention?"

"You could have tried *not* using a dog nose!"

She looked like she was trying not to laugh, which infuriated him. Shirtless and covered in engine grease, he knew he probably looked like some hick yokel, and the fact that she looked like a spring breeze wasn't helping.

"It's unsafe!" he barked. "Get out of the garage!"

"There's no need to yell," she said and turned to walk out to the yard with her nose firmly in the air.

Angrily, he climbed out of the pit and yanked on his t-shirt. Ten to one, the girl needed a tire change or something equally stupid.

"Well?" he demanded, looking around the lot as he came out into the sunshine.

"Well, what?" she asked, looking up at him.

"Your car. Where is it?"

"Out on the road, next to the sign that says one mile to Luckless."

"Did you run out of gas?" he asked sarcastically.

"No," she said, looking angry in her turn. "It's a vintage airstream. It broke down."

"Ah, the preferred vehicle of hipsters," said Jordan, folding his arms across his chest.

"Can you help me or not?" she demanded, anger flushing her cheeks.

"Unfortunately, I cannot. The tow truck is out at Beauford's pulling… It's on another job." There was no way he was mentioning Beauford's cow to this city slicker.

She took a deep breath, which did lovely things to her cleavage that he tried not to notice.

"So, how long will I have to wait?"

"I don't know," he said. "Leave your number, and we'll call you when it's back."

"Leave my number? Where am I supposed to go?"

"Go sit at one of the charming café's in town." He jerked his thumb in the direction of the road. "I'm sure Yelp can direct you to something *off the beaten path*."

"I have a dog. You can't just go into a café with a dog!"

It was a reasonable objection, although he knew several of the café owners would be fine with the cute little terrier sitting politely at the girl's feet. But admitting that made it sound like Luckless was littered with unprofessional restaurateurs.

"Try Sir Barkington's Bed & Breakfast," he said. "Straight down Main and turn on Orchard."

"All right," she said, her lips compressed into a thin line. She looked like she was barely hanging onto her temper. She reached into her bag, pulled out a fat Sharpie-type pen, gave it a firm click, and then looked at him as if waiting for something. "You're going to need my number," she said as if she were explaining things to a five-year-old. "What am I writing it on?"

He grimaced and looked around for something to write on but saw nothing. She made a disgusted noise and grabbed his hand. With firm strokes, she scrawled out her number into his palm.

"Maybe this will make sure you remember to call." She wrote her name and underlined it, ending with a forceful jab.

"Come on, Skipper," she said to the dog and turned on her heel, leaving Jordan standing in the yard with the sinking feeling that he had just given the world's worst customer service to the gorgeous—he looked at his palm—Simone.

"Michelle is going to kill me," he said to the empty lot.

CHAPTER 2
This Year's Dreams

Simone

Simone stormed along Main Street with long, angry strides. Which would have been a lot more satisfying except that Skipper kept pausing to smell the plantings around the spindly trees that had been nestled into new bump-outs along the sidewalk.

"How dare he? I would have apologized if he hadn't been so—" Skipper yanked her to a stop by a tree, and she waved her fists around her head in fury. "Rude!" She looked up and realized the light poles had all been decorated with charming little flags and flower baskets. Had she not been in mid-fury she might have taken a picture.

She made it another half block before Skipper pulled her to a stop again.

"If I thought for a second there was another garage in this stupid town, I would go there! He thinks just because he's all hot and sweaty and built like…" She trailed off, picturing what the mechanic had been built like. "You know what? We don't need to dwell on the fact that he looks straight off the cover of a romance novel. Because that is…" Simone pictured his abs and sandy brown hair sprinkled with gold highlights and that hilariously adorable smear of grease. "Not really the point. The point is that he was rude, mean, sarcastic, and not even good at his job! *That* is the point!"

Skipper looked like he agreed with her while he peed on a tree.

"Skipper, that is brand new landscaping. You are not helping."

Skipper did not look like he cared about landscaping. She pulled Skipper away from killing any more plantings and went to the corner, only to realize that she had not been paying attention, and she had no idea if she had passed Orchard already or not. She looked around, hoping to see some sort of sign or landmark.

"Are you lost, dear?" asked a friendly woman coming out of a bank. She wore a gingham check shirt over a comfortably plump frame, with capri-length jeans and sandals. She reminded Simone so forcefully of Colorado summers and every mom of every childhood friend that she felt a wave of homesickness.

"I'm trying to go to Sir Barkington's," said Simone hesitantly.

"Ah, of course! Going to see your doggy friends?" she asked, leaning down to scratch Skipper's ears. "Caleb really is the best. You just need to go another block up to Orchard there and turn left. Can't miss it."

"Thank you," said Simone.

"Are you in town for the big event?" asked the woman, standing up with a smile.

"Big event?"

"The wine festival! We're ever so excited. The Amante Winery is hosting The Decanter Classic this year. It's internationally recognized, you know. We've got wineries coming from Paris, Australia, South America, and all over the States."

"I don't know much about wine. Is that why everything is so pretty?" Simone gestured at the street, and the woman rolled her eyes.

"Well, it certainly helped. But the Mayor has been trying to get this roadway improvement done for six years. Finally happened. It does look pretty, doesn't it? It's been the mayor's hobby horse to improve walkability for a stronger downtown core by widening the sidewalks and narrowing the streets. I hate to admit it, but she was right. It's improved parking, brought speeds down, and I *do* think people are walking more. But it was *quite* the contentious issue at the town hall meetings, let me tell you."

"Oh," said Simone. "That's great that everyone cares about the town so much."

"Doesn't everyone?" asked the woman with a shrug.

"No, I've been to every state in the Union," said Simone. "Trust me. Not everyone cares."

"Really? Every state? Well, that's impressive. Did you fly?"

"No, I drove to most of them," said Simone.

"You and your little doggy?"

"I picked up Skipper in South Dakota," said Simone.

"He's adorable. Yes, he is!" The woman bent down to scrub at Skipper's ears again. Skipper looked like he thought this was his due. "What a fun adventure! How bold of you! I think I've been to three states and that's about it. How did you come up with that idea?"

Simone floundered. She ought to be practiced up at the question, but almost no one directly asked why she was visiting, and when they did, she usually said something simple about being on a road trip. "My Dad died," she blurted out. "I promised him I would take some of his ashes to all the states."

"Ah, honey!" The woman reached out and hugged Simone tightly before setting her back on her feet. "I'm so sorry for your loss. I'm Linda, by the way. How wonderful of you to honor your father that way."

"I'm Simone," said Simone, blushing. She felt silly laying out her tragedy for this woman and even sillier for feeling so bolstered by her kind words. "Thank you. This is my last stop. Dad was born here, so he wanted the last bit to be here."

"Oh my goodness! That is lovely," said Linda, putting her hand over her heart. "What was your Dad's name?"

"Charles Laurent," said Simone. "I think they moved away when Dad was fifteen or so."

"Now wait, that rings a bell. He had a sister named Juliette? Pretty girl with dark hair."

"Yes," said Simone, surprised. "Yes, that's them." Simone smiled and stopped her commentary there, not wanting to add that she didn't know much about Aunt Juliette. Juliette and her father's relationship had been difficult and icy because Charles had not approved of Juliette's marriage, and even after she had been widowed, the connection had remained strained. Only when Charles had gotten sick did Simone come to be on friendly terms with her aunt.

"Juliette was a year or so behind me. Everyone was in love with her." Linda's eyes twinkled. "You'd think a tragedy had struck the male population when she left. I'm so sorry to hear about your father."

"Thanks," said Simone.

"Do you want me to give you a ride to Sir Barkington's? You two look hot."

"We're all right," said Simone. "I wouldn't want to bother you."

"Don't be silly. My car's right here." She gestured to a big boat of a Cadillac parked two spaces up. "It's only two blocks out of my way. I drive that much extra when I stop paying attention and start singing to the radio."

Simone laughed. "Well…" She looked down at Skipper, who had collapsed into the minuscule shade of a plant and was panting. "If you don't mind a dog in the car."

"Not a bit," said Linda cheerfully. "Come along."

Once Simone was settled into the plush seats of the Cadillac with Skipper beside her, Linda blasted the AC and let the Caddie meander out onto the street. No one seemed to be in a hurry to go anywhere, and a car actually paused and waved to let her into traffic. It was only a few minutes later that Linda pulled up in front of a bright yellow Victorian house with deep magenta trim.

"Oh my," said Simone. "I guess you were right. That house is difficult to miss."

Linda laughed. "The neighbors were not fans when he first started painting it, but Caleb had them roped and tied before they were even out of the chute. The colors are historically accurate and one hundred percent in compliance with the historic house ordinance. Plus, I do believe he bribed them with cookies and bourbon. And then there are the puppies that are frequently found rolling across the lawn. I mean, really… who can say no to that?"

"Cookies, bourbon, and puppies? Isn't that the definition of heaven?" asked Simone.

"You might be right," said Linda with a laugh.

Simone got out of the car, profusely thanking Linda for the ride, which the older woman waved away with an easy smile before driving off with a cheerful toot of the car horn. Simone stood on the front walk and looked up at the wide porch where a basset hound sat with prim prima donna feet by a table already set with a pitcher of iced tea.

Unable to resist, Simone lifted her camera and took a picture. The entire scene felt as if it had been laid out by a set designer to radiate charm.

The Bassett hound let out a baying woof as she took another picture, and she realized he was wearing a calico bowtie.

"Skipper," said Simone, "you've got competition. This dog is about the cutest thing ever."

"Well, thank you," said a man coming out of the house. He had brown curly hair and wore a vest and a bowtie that matched the dogs. "Anyone who compliments Sir Barkington the Third is welcome here. Come on up to the porch and have some tea. The cookies will be out shortly. The dog and human kind."

Jordan

"Hey, Michelle," said Jordan, picking up his phone.

"Hey, did anyone call in? I'm on the way back from Beauford's, and there's an adorable little airstream parked by the side of the road."

"Uh, yeah," said Jordan, looking guiltily at his palm. "Simone. She walked in and said she needed a tow because it broke down. I've got her number."

"She's not there?"

"No. I, uh, sent her to Sir Barkington's. She had a dog with her."

"Uh, OK, I guess. You couldn't have handed her one of the Vogue's in the waiting room and given the dog some water?"

"Well, I didn't know how long you'd be gone," said Jordan, trying not to sound like he was whining. "And George called and said he needed some help at the winery."

"Jordan! For crying out loud!" snapped Michelle. "You need to stop saying yes. You're the manager at the winery. You can't jump every time someone calls."

"Martinez called in because his kids are sick. What else am I supposed to do?" snapped Jordan.

"Hire someone else. Or let the work go until Monday."

"The grapes come when the grapes come," said Jordan defensively.

"Yeah, well, how come when the grapes aren't coming in, you're still working?"

Jordan sighed, rubbed his head, and almost instantly regretted it—the grease was still in his hair. "We can't afford another full-time person right now, and I'm the only one without a family and kids. I pick up the slack because I have to."

"Everyone is too used to relying on you," said Michelle. "You need to set some boundaries."

"Can we talk about this later," said Jordan. "I have to get to work. I left Simone's number on the pad by the phone."

"OK, fine," said Michelle. "Come to dinner tomorrow night, and we can talk then."

Jordan grinned. "Sure," he promised easily, knowing that talking would never happen. Michelle's house was a tornado of children and sports. Michelle's husband, Graham, was a teacher and basketball coach at the local high school. Dinner at Michelle's was going to involve playing horse with his niece and nephew while Graham grilled, and Michelle tried to complete a thought between the yells of her children. "Hey, um, about Simone."

"What about her?" asked Michelle.

"She might be a bit ticked off at me?" Jordan winced at his own words.

"And why would she be ticked at you?"

"Well, I didn't hear the bell in the office and then she came into the garage. I got startled, and I kind of yelled at her."

"Jordan!"

"I'm sorry! But she made me drop the whole box of socket wrenches."

"So, she walks all the way into town at five on a hot day, and instead of being greeted with sympathy and a glass of water, you yelled at her and made her walk further?"

Jordan groaned. "It sounds bad when you put it like that."

"This poor woman must think you're a total jerk."

"Probably," said Jordan. "She looked kind of peeved when she left. But it's fine."

"How is it fine?"

"She was going to be peeved anyway. She had hipster tourist

written all over her. We were never going to live up to expectations."

"But we didn't have to live down to them, now did we?" demanded Michelle. "Really, Jordan!"

"Sorry!"

"I'm going to ban you from talking to any customers ever. I honestly don't know how you sell wine."

"I don't sell wine. I *make* wine. Other people who have social skills are responsible for the selling."

Michelle snorted in laughter. "Fair enough. All right. I'm going to hang up and get this car loaded. I'll call this poor Simone woman and try and apologize when I get back to the shop."

"I really am sorry," said Jordan.

"Whatever," said Michelle. "See you tomorrow."

Simone

"Well, oh my goodness," said Caleb Bennett as Simone finished telling the extended version of how she came to be in Luckless. "I am so sorry for the loss of your father, but you have just been having adventure after adventure."

Simone laughed. "It felt like that for a while there."

"But it's stopped feeling like that?" he asked, his keen brown eyes scrutinizing her face.

"I don't know. I got back from Hawaii, and somehow, everything stopped feeling like a vacation and started feeling a little more like hard work. The bank account getting lower and lower hasn't helped. Now, I just want to be done and settled back home. But it's not like I have anything back in Colorado to return to. I sold the house to pay off all of Dad's medical bills and my student loans and finance this trip. Basically, I'll be going back and finding a friend who will let me plug in the motorhome at their place and looking for a job. Which sounds depressing."

"Ah, yes. The dreaded real job. I got rid of mine, and I've never been happier. I walked out of Google three years ago and I cannot but think it was the best decision I've ever made. What about you? What's your passion? Photography?" He waggled a finger at Simone's camera resting on the table next to her iced tea.

"Yes," said Simone with a laugh. "I can't believe I'm telling you all of this."

"That's my secret weapon," said Caleb, topping up her iced tea. "I'm highly skilled in ferreting out interesting life stories. Why don't you do something with photography?"

"I'd love to, but it doesn't exactly pay the bills. I could do something in marketing, but I don't have any connections, so I keep surfing the job boards and getting depressed because I don't have any work history. I have a degree in Communication, but Dad got sick right after I graduated, and I never had a chance to get a job with it. Now, I feel like I'm behind everyone else. I just know I will end up working some horrible retail job."

"Defeatist thinking!" cried Caleb, raising a stern finger.

"It's hard not to fall into defeatist thinking with only Skipper to talk to," said Simone. "When I first left home, I was so glad not to have to talk to anyone or answer the question *how are you* again. But now, at state fifty, I'm starting to talk to any random person on the street or bed and breakfast owner I can find."

Caleb laughed. "There are worse people to talk to," he said. "But yes, I can see you have definitely reached a point where you need a vacation from your vacation. And perhaps you will say I'm prejudiced, but there are worse places than Luckless to take a break."

"Oh, I'm not staying," said Simone. "I'm sorry for talking

your ear off, but I'm not even sure I'm staying the night here. I just need to get the motorhome back and find a good place to leave Dad's ashes and then I'm off to Colorado. And then, hopefully… this will be the year I get to focus on making my life mine. And also, hopefully, the jerk at Ryan's Garage will call soon."

"The jerk?" Caleb looked surprised.

"The sweaty mechanic who yelled at me just because Skipper surprised him and maybe made him knock over a box of tools."

"Oh, dear!"

"I'd been ringing the bell for like five solid minutes, so I went out to the garage and apparently the mechanic didn't hear us and, boom, over went the tools. I would have apologized, except he read me the riot act and kicked me out of the garage. He said the tow truck was out somewhere, and he'd call when it got back."

"Hm," said Caleb. "That really doesn't sound like Stewie."

"Tall guy, brown hair?" said Simone, struggling not to mention the six-pack abs as that seemed non-supportive of her complaints.

"Hm," repeated Caleb, looking puzzled. "Well, I'm sure they'll call soon. But if they don't, then I think you should stay for dinner."

"Oh, I can't stay for dinner," said Simone, distressed. "I've already taken up all your time and tea."

Caleb laughed. "You do not understand," he said, patting her hand. "I have left Google and the rat race behind so that when I feel like sitting on my porch and inviting passers-by to dinner I can. There are no *have-to's* or time-tables. Unless it's cookies or breakfast. In which case, the bell must be answered. But other than that, Sir Barkington and I do as we please."

Sir Barkington, sound asleep on the porch next to Skipper, let out a woof upon hearing his name and woke himself up. He looked around as if startled by his surroundings.

"Silly old boy," said Caleb, bending down to rub Sir Barkington's floppy ears. "It's why I'm not looking forward to next week."

"Next week?"

"The wine event. I'm all booked up with doggos. I don't know how I'm going to look after all the poochies, let alone the people. My precious free time will evaporate like the dew. Not to mention that my teenage helper has decided to do the unthinkable and abscond to Disneyland with her family during my hour of need. Ungrateful ragamuffin!"

Simone laughed. "Youth of today," she said with a mocking headshake.

"Exactly! So you must stay to dinner and hear me complain about them."

"I don't know," Simone began to protest but was cut off by her phone.

"Speak of the devil?" asked Caleb, and she nodded as she grabbed it off the table and swiped it to green.

"Hello," she said. "This is Simone."

"Hi Simone," said a pleasant female voice. "This is Michelle Ryan over at Ryan's Garage."

"Oh," said Simone, feeling surprised that the Ryan of Ryan's Garage was a woman and then guilty for assuming it was a man. "Hi. Thanks for calling me back," she said. "Um, my motorhome is out on the road."

"Yeah, I brought it in already."

"Oh!" Simone felt relieved at this quick movement. She'd been expecting more horrible service. "That's great."

"Yeah, I'm afraid that was the easy part. I went ahead and had a look at it once I got it into the shop. It looks like someone tore out the engine and replaced it with a modern one at some point?"

"Yeah, my Dad did it to make it more fuel-efficient. Otherwise, it felt like we were just one giant silver pollution bullet."

Michelle chuckled. "Yeah, I hear that. It was a good rebuild. But in order to make it fit with the existing vehicle, it looks like he had to get a bit creative."

"Creative sounds expensive," said Simone, knowing that her voice had dropped and hating herself for sounding like a child.

"Yeah… Sorry. But to get her running again, it's going to be about fourteen hundred in parts and another four hundred in labor."

"Eighteen hundred dollars?" asked Simone, her eyes filling with tears as she did the math.

"Yeah, I'm really sorry. Um, what do you want to do?"

"I don't know," said Simone. "Um…"

"Jordan said you were over at Sir Barkington's? Do you want to maybe think on it overnight and get back to me? I can't start right away anyway. I'll have to order parts in the morning."

"Um, OK," said Simone. "Thanks."

"Eighteen hundred dollars," said Simone, looking at Caleb. "I can't afford that. I could practically find a used car for that. But I need the motorhome to live in once I get back to Colorado. What am I going to do?"

"You will give me a moment to think," said Caleb, steepling his fingers. "This is what I used to do," he said, unsteepling and giving her a reassuring nod. "I did job placement at Google. I will now go into the mental rolodex and I will consider."

"Oh," said Simone, who hadn't realized that job placement was a superpower. She waited while Caleb ruminated with his eyes closed. Skipper gave her a look, and Simone shrugged. She didn't know what to think either.

"Very well," said Caleb, taking a breath and opening his eyes. "I have a plan. You will stay for dinner, and then I will put you in the Lavender Room."

"That's not a good plan," said Simone. "I can't afford that

either."

"It is free because you will help me with the dogs and the people while you are staying here. And then on the morrow—"

"The morrow?" asked Simone skeptically.

"Don't interrupt me when I'm being grandiose. On the morrow, thou shalt get thee to the winery."

"Why the winery?" asked Simone, amused by her new friend's pompous tone.

"Because they need an Events Assistant for the Decanter Classic. You should be able to earn a good chunk of that eighteen hundred dollars in the next couple of weeks."

"That might work," said Simone hesitantly. "And maybe my aunt could chip in a few hundred dollars. She did say she felt like she owed me for taking care of Dad's funeral."

"There you go," said Caleb with a nod.

Simone chewed her lip as she considered. "I really do hate asking for money."

"Do not ask," suggested Caleb. "Simply call and tell her your sad tale of woe. I bet she ponies up voluntarily."

"Caleb," said Simone, "I think maybe you need to cut back on the Masterpiece Theater."

"Darling girl, I do believe everyone else simply needs to watch more."

Jordan slammed down the case of full wine bottles, earning a startled glare from George. George was a balding man who compensated for a bare scalp with an enormous mustache. He had been at the winery almost as long as Jordan had been alive. He tended to view Jordan's promotion to head enologist and manager of the winery with amusement and still periodically tried to order him around. Or, in this case, call him in to do all the last-minute odd jobs that had to get done. But Jordan was genuinely starting to think Michelle was right—those jobs didn't need to be done by him.

He knew he needed to assert himself more and move into the manager position more fully, but it was difficult. Mateo had hired him right out of college, and now, at thirty-three, he was having trouble getting the staff to view him as anything other than the college kid with a head stuffed full of book knowledge about wine. He knew it would be easier to get respect if he went to a different winery. He'd received a few casually hinted-at invitations from some of the local brands. But his home was here in Luckless, and moving to a new town, let alone a new winery, seemed like running out on his family.

"This is ridiculous," said Jordan. "I cannot be toting wine cases at six in the evening. Not only do I have better things to do with my Saturday night—"

"Like what?" asked George. "You haven't had a date in a year."

"Anything is better than this," said Jordan. "Also, literally, I have more important things to do *here*. I should be testing the pH balance on the Rosé. Why are we doing this again?"

"Because we need to get the wine bottled before the Classic and Gabe bailed, and Martinez can't because his kid got sick and his wife is working night-shift at the hospital, so he has to stay home. Which means that Martinez isn't here to tote the wine or cover for Gabe, and now we're toting the wine and running the bottling machine."

"Why does Gabe always bail?" demanded Jordan.

"He doesn't always bail," protested George and then looked

guilty. "OK, he bails a lot. But what am I supposed to do? If we fire Gabe then half my picking crew is going to give me the hairy eyeball."

"I don't know why anyone would worry about field workers not having a union," said Jordan. "All you have to do is marry into the Gonzalez family and—bam—union."

"The dues are too high," said George with a chuckle.

"Wine is not Gabe's passion. He needs to get a job better suited to his talents," said Jordan firmly.

"What talents would those be?" asked George drily.

"He has talents," said Jordan with a sigh. "He's actually pretty smart when you talk to him. But answering phones and bottling or doing anything really outdoorsy is not his forte. Honestly, he should go into politics."

"Hey! He's a good kid!"

"I'm not saying he's not. I'm saying he's smart, very persuasive, and has a knack for talking to everyone and talking them into things they don't want to do. For instance… you and me, toting boxes on a Saturday night."

"Oh. Yeah, I see what you mean. Yeah, something where he negotiates with other people's money for a living would be good," agreed George. "You know what we really need?"

"Don't say it," said Jordan.

"Another person would be nice," said George, and Jordan groaned. "What? We've got the event coming up next week, and we're already scrambling. What are we going to do when it's actually here? We don't even need a wine person. We need someone who can do all the stuff you millennials are supposed to be good at. All the social media and marketing stuff. And then we need someone who can pitch in, pour wine, and drive trucks. Why can't we have that person?"

"You don't think I've made that case to Mateo?" demanded

Jordan.

"Well, what did he say?"

"He said no. Money's tight," said Jordan. "If we can win an award at the Classic, then it will boost our profile and we can start putting some marketing dollars behind that. But until we've got something to push, Mateo won't approve the extra money."

George let out a grumpy sigh. Then he looked over his shoulder and around the loading dock as if they weren't the only two on the premises. "Man to man, Jordan, what are the odds of winning something at the Classic?"

Jordan found himself unable to stop the grin that spread across his face. "Nothing's a sure bet, George, but I swear that this is the year. This wine is… it's really, really good."

George sighed. "I really want this for the old man. Ten years without a major award is a long dry spell. I know it's not until next week, but I'm so nervous already."

"How do you think I feel?" demanded Jordan.

"Sorry," said George, flashing a smile under his mustache. "It's going to be great. The wine is going to win, and everything is going to be great."

"Keep saying it, George," said Jordan. "I need to hear it."

CHAPTER 3
Resumes

Simone

Simone came out of the airstream and into the garage parking lot. Caleb, leaning against his Smart car, looked her pantsuit over.

"Job hunting approved?" asked Simone nervously. "Everything else I own is jeans."

Caleb wrinkled his nose. "If this was the city, it would be great, but it's not. I feel like you're going to alienate people by looking too fancy. What have you got in the way of a dress?"

"Well…" Simone mentally rummaged through her minuscule wardrobe. "Oh, wait. I've got one. Hold on."

Simone went back inside and pulled open the tiny closet that contained the three clothing items she didn't want to fold.

The early morning visit to Ryan's Garage to collect Simone's things from the motorhome had been met with equanimity by Michelle Ryan, who turned out to be a thirty-something woman in an ancient-looking *Ryan's Garage* t-shirt and blue mechanics overalls with the sleeves tied around her waist. Michelle Ryan had been friendly and very polite, probably trying to make up for her jerk mechanic, who was nowhere in sight this morning. The plan was to collect Simone's clothes and toiletries and then try and find a job somewhere in town. Caleb was being an amazing help. She suspected that he was a little bit bored and she was his new favorite project.

Simone hung up the white button-up and pulled on the blue cotton dress. It was knee-length, bright blue, and if she put a cardigan over it, with the close-toed flats she'd worn to the funeral, she probably looked office-y enough.

She went back out to see Caleb, and he beamed. "Blue is your color. If I can't get you a job in that outfit, I have utterly lost my touch. All right, grab your gear, and then we'll pop up to the winery."

Michelle came out of the office, a mug of coffee in her hand, and looked Simone over. "What's the occasion?" she asked, looking like dresses were a foreign concept.

"Well," said Simone, feeling embarrassed but also a little bit annoyed at Michelle for not immediately connecting the dots. "I don't have the money to pay for the repairs, so Caleb is helping me get a job."

Michelle winced. "You look great," she said. "I'm sorry about the money. Maybe I can knock a bit off the labor."

"I will pay the entire bill," said Simone firmly. "You have the right to make a living. I just wasn't budgeting for this kind of expense before I got back to Colorado."

"I figure that someone will need help during the Decanter Classic next week," said Caleb cheerfully. "We'll get the cash together in no time."

"I'm sure you will," said Michelle, smiling. "I'll order the parts today. We'll have you back on your way before you know it. Your dad did an excellent job on the retrofit. It should be quick to put back together."

"I'm just glad he got it done in time," said Simone, patting the turquoise accent stripe on the silver motorhome.

"He had a road trip planned for a long time?" asked Michelle cheerfully.

"Yeah, I guess he did," said Simone, with a shrug, not wanting to talk about it.

There was an awkward moment, and Simone thought Caleb was making some sort of hand gestures behind her because Michelle's eyebrows went up in confusion. But when Simone turned to look at him, he simply smiled at her.

"Well, we should get going and make the rounds," said Caleb. "Wish us luck, Michelle."

"Good luck!" agreed Michelle. "Let me know if I can help."

"Will do! Into the car with you, Ms. Laurent. Let's hit the mean streets of Luckless!"

Michelle chuckled and shook her head as Simone and Caleb got in the car.

"All right," said Caleb, easing the tiny car onto the street. "Off to the winery. We'll pop in and talk to the owner. I bet he'll snap you up. He was complaining just last week that Jordan and the crew were running around like crazy people. But if that doesn't work, I have three other people in mind."

"Who's Jordan?" asked Simone.

"Darling boy. You'll love him. He's Michelle's brother and the Amante enologist. That's the person who makes wines. And personally, I believe him to be a genius."

Simone laughed. "A genius?"

"Yes! I'm quite serious! He has mysterious ways with grapes. His small blends are devastatingly delicious. I have high hopes they'll take home a medal in the Classic this year and maybe even the Best in Show cup."

"I shall have to learn more about wine," said Simone. "I mean, we drank wine at home, but it was just whatever Dad liked. Dad and Grandpa used to get into huge fights about it, though."

"Over wine? Well, in general, that's understandable, but what, in specific, were they arguing about?"

"Well, my family emigrated from France in, like, the 1920s, and that was really, really, really important to Grandpa. You would have thought Dad committed some sort of cardinal sin the one time he tried to serve an Italian wine at Christmas. It was pretty epic."

Caleb chuckled. "Sounds like it could be a rather fraught at holidays."

"No, not really. Just loud. They liked to argue." Simone's phone rang. "It's my aunt. She's calling me back. I thought she'd call back later."

"Just answer it," said Caleb. "I'm sure it will be fine."

Simone sighed and did as she was told. "Hi, Juliette!"

"Hey, sweetie," said Juliette. "I got your message. You made it to Luckless?"

"Well," said Simone, clearing her throat, "I made it *almost* to Luckless. The motorhome broke down just outside out of town."

"Oh no! Are you all right?"

"Yes, I found a wonderful bed and breakfast called Sir Barkington's, and the owner, Caleb, is helping me find a job." Caleb beamed at her description.

"I'm sorry…" There was a pause as Juliette seemed to huff a bit into the phone. "What?"

"Well, the motorhome is going to be almost two thousand dollars to repair, and I need it for when I get back to Colorado, and I can't really afford that kind of cash, so I'm going to get a job for a few weeks."

"I don't think I quite understand why you need it when you get back to Colorado. You're not planning on living it, are you? Aren't you going to be staying in your house?"

"Um," said Simone. "I just need it to…" Simone floundered for a way to say that she'd already sold the house but couldn't come up with anything. "Anyway, I need to get the cash together, so I'm going to get a job." Total topic avoidance, but maybe Juliette wouldn't notice.

"Well, but I can give you the money."

"No, I couldn't have you pay for everything," said Simone. Caleb glared at her, and she grimaced back.

"Well, I can pay for some of it," said Juliette. "I know you had a lot of expenses with your father's medical bills and the funeral. I can pay for half at least."

"Um… That would be great!" said Simone, feeling both relieved and guilty.

"OK, well, tell me where to send it and I can get a check out to you. Or I can probably figure out one of those fancy online things."

"I'm on my way to the winery," Simone said. "Caleb thinks they can probably use help there because there's a big wine event next week."

"The Amante Winery?" asked Juliette, sounding a bit breathless.

"Yes," said Simone. "They're hosting the wine thing next week. So they're probably going to need help."

"That sounds likely," said Juliette. "What's the town like? I never went back, you know, after we moved. I'm kind of dying to know if everything's changed."

"Well, they put in flowers and trees on Main Street. And the fountain outside of town is gorgeous."

"Did you toss a coin to Cupid?" asked Juliette, sounding amused.

Simone laughed. "I did, actually. I met a nice man named Mateo, who gave me a penny to toss in."

"Mateo?" repeated Juliette.

"Nice older guy. He told me all about the fountain. So far, I have to say that except for the mechanic, everyone has been really nice."

"That's Luckless for you," said Juliette. "I really ought to come back and visit."

"Linda remembered you," said Simone. "Don't ask me her last name. But she said all the boys cried when you left."

"I don't think quite *all* the boys cried," said Juliette drily. "But maybe I could come back. I don't know…"

"You should. Anyway, it looks like we're turning off for the winery, and I should talk to Caleb about how not to freak out and what to say. I'll text you Sir Barkington's address in a bit."

"OK, dear," said Juliette. "I'll call again tonight and see how it went."

"OK, bye!"

"Bye, love you!"

The line went dead, and Simone stared at her phone. "We were never close growing up," she said to Caleb. "So it's kind of weird to hear her say *I love you*."

"But it's kind of nice, isn't it?" asked Caleb.

"Yeah," said Simone, looking out the window at the quickly approaching winery, "It really is."

Juliette

Juliette Laurent hung up the phone and looked around the living room of the modern condo that was currently her home. Bright fall sunlight was streaming through the windows, showing off Portland to its best advantage.

"She didn't answer my question about the house," Juliette said to the phone.

There was a knock on her door, and she got up to answer it.

"Julie!" trilled her neighbor, throwing up her hands in delight. "You will never guess who we saw at the grocery store!"

"Who?" asked Juliette, hugging Maxine.

"Dan Forelle. You remember him—he has a boat." Maxine bustled into the condo, tossing her purse onto the kitchen counter and taking off her sunglasses.

"Yes," said Juliette. "I remember Dan. And what I remember about Dan is that he has exactly two topics of conversation—his boat and his job."

"Well, he is suddenly single and was hinting around that I could pass on his number to you. Uh, I see wine glasses, but..." Maxine pointed significantly at the wine glasses that Juliette had gotten out in preparation for Maxine's visit.

"Go sit down. But why would I want a guy who can talk for a solid hour about insurance adjustment?" asked Juliette, going into the kitchen.

"Well, because it might be nice for you to go out with someone on a date, for one thing," said Maxine. "It's been a while."

"I don't mind being single," said Juliette, going to the wine rack and pulling out a bottle. She stared at the bottle in dissatisfaction and then, after a moment of indecision, put it back and reached in for the wine she really wanted.

"I know you don't mind, but wouldn't it be nice to have a little company every once and a while? Aren't you ready for a change?" asked Maxine wistfully.

"Yes," said Juliette, staring at the bottle with the blue and silver Amante label. "I think I am."

"Oh, that looks yummy. What is it—a Barbera? Branching out into Italian? Don't stand there staring at it. Pour! I didn't retire so I could *not* day drink."

Juliette laughed. "I'm pouring, I'm pouring. You know," she said, digging in the drawer for the corkscrew. "I've actually been wishing I could change a few things for a while now."

"Like what?" asked Maxine, seating herself at the bar counter. She took off her sunhat and ran a hand through her short red curls.

"Oh, the past mostly."

"Too late to do that," said Maxine.

"Yes, but well, what if it's not too late to change the future?" Juliette popped the cork and reached for the aerator.

"What does that mean?" asked Maxine, looking skeptical.

"I just talked to my niece."

"The sweet girl on the huge road trip?"

"Yes, Simone. She was heading for Luckless Washington. That's where Charles and I were born. But her motorhome broke down."

"Oh no! Is she all right?"

"Yes, but it sounds like it will be a lot of money to repair. She was talking about getting a job to pay for the repairs. She wouldn't let me pay for it. And I was wondering if I shouldn't fly out there and rescue her."

"It did seem like the poor thing could use a bit of mothering," said Maxine sympathetically. "She has had to be quite independent, what with taking care of her father during his illness."

"Yes, but also…"

"But what?" demanded Maxine, accepting her glass of wine.

"I always swore I wouldn't go back to Luckless," said Juliette, taking a slow sip of wine. "But lately, I've been wondering if I was a fool. Young, dumb, and too stubborn for my own good."

"Young, dumb, and in love?" asked Maxine, looking at her knowingly over the rim of her glass.

"Maybe," said Juliette.

"Is he still there?"

"Simone said he was," said Juliette, blushing slightly. "But for all I know, he's married and hasn't thought about me in years. I don't know. Should I go?"

"Honey," said Maxine with a wry smile, "at our age, you only get one shot at a second chance. If it were me, I'd be on the first plane out of town."

Simone

Simone slowly got out of Caleb's car and examined the winery. From the road, the Amante winery looked like a two-story neo-classical building with wide columns built of warm yellow sandstone. In front, a spacious courtyard full of scattered tables and umbrellas gave the impression of a European estate waiting for guests to arrive. Behind the main house, she could see the rooflines of two large warehouse structures. There was no disguising their functionality, but even they had old-world barn touches.

"That's the owner's house," said Caleb, pointing down the road to a house that, while smaller than the winery building, looked similar in architecture.

On the far side of the gravel parking lot, amongst a grove of poplar trees, was the most American-looking structure on the property – a barn of gray faded wood.

"What's that building over there?" she asked, pointing to the barn.

"I believe they refer to that as Jordan's Bat Cave," said Caleb. "They say that Jordan comes up with all the best wines in that building. It's not included on the tour, so personally, I choose to believe that it comes with a fireman's pole, bat-mobile, and a red phone to the mayor. Although, I did hear his nephew once say that Jordan kept an old PacMan game and jar full of suckers in there."

Simone laughed. "Jordan sounds fun."

"He's a sweetheart," said Caleb. "You'll like him."

Simone followed Caleb into the tasting room. It had a large square brick red tile floor that reminded her of her childhood kitchen. There was even the warm hint of garlic spicing the air.

"I'll pop out and see who's around," said Caleb. "Wait here."

Simone nodded and continued to look around. The heavy dark wood bar took up the far wall and there were tables around the floor. The overall feeling was cozy, which should have been hard to achieve in such a large room. She liked it and started picking out which angles she would photograph a party here. If she did the lighting right, she could give it all the intimate feeling of a smoky jazz bar.

There was a clunk and the sound of what might have been an expletive from the other side of the door near the bar.

"Did you need some help?" asked Simone, opening the door.

"Yes," said a good-looking boy with boy band-level hair tousle. He looked about nineteen or twenty, and he was carrying a box of wine bottles in his arms. "Possibly with my spatial awareness. I totally ran into the edge of the door and took a crate of wine in the chin."

"Oh no!" Simone grabbed the wine out of his arms, and the boy rubbed his chin with a groaning noise. "Are you all right?"

"I think I'll make it. Can you pop that on the bar? And maybe hold the door for me when I come back?"

"Sure," said Simone, hoisting the wine box onto the bar.

"Thanks. I clearly cannot be trusted to open my own doors." He gave Simone a wink and then disappeared back down the hallway he'd come out of. Simone let the door swing shut while she waited for Caleb or the boy to return, but then found she was standing by the door feeling a bit silly with nothing to occupy her while she waited.

"Well, if it isn't the girl who's owed a penny's worth of the love," said a pleasant voice, and she turned to see her friend from the fountain walk into the room.

"Oh, hello! You're here!"

"Yes, and so are you. Simone, wasn't it?"

"Yes, Simone Laurent," said Simone, coming forward and offering her hand.

"Laurent, did you say?" He asked, smiling as he shook her hand. "Are you related to Charles and Juliette?"

"Yes, Charles was my dad," said Simone. "Did you know them?"

"A bit." She thought his smile stretched even wider. "How is the motorhome?"

"Not good," said Simone, grimacing. "It's going to be really expensive to repair, so Caleb is taking me around like his favorite show pony in the hopes of getting a temp job during the wine festival thing."

"Show pony?" asked Mateo with a laugh.

"If I braided my hair, I'm sure there would be a resemblance," said Simone, grinning. There was a clunk in the hall, so Simone went to open it for the boy.

"Thanks, you're a real lifesaver," said the boy, pulling a dolly loaded with wine crates. He backed through the door, carefully trying to avoid the door frame. "Or at least a wall saver. I think I barely drive one of these better than I drive my car."

"No tickets on these, though," said Simone, and the boy chuckled.

He off-loaded the crates onto the floor and managed to wheel the dolly back through the door in one swoop. "One more trip. Be right back," he called from the hall without a backward glance.

"Anyway," said Simone, going back to Mateo, "my aunt said she'd pay for some of the repairs, and Caleb says I can stay with him if I help him with the dogs. So I just need to get something that will fill in the rest. He thought the winery might need some help."

"Well, yes," said Mateo. "That's true. Everyone seems to be

run quite ragged. They're even depending on the help of random visitors to get through the door."

Simone laughed. "It's just the door. I don't mind helping."

"Helping is excellent, but what kind of job did you really want?" asked Mateo.

"Oh, anything really. But I have a BA in Communication, so I do have marketing skills. Not that I can prove it."

"A marketing person who doesn't mind helping would indeed be useful during an event," said Mateo thoughtfully.

"I also have my Commercial Driver's License," said Simone. "Because of the motorhome. I thought that might be useful, too. I don't know what for, but at this point, I'll take whatever job I can find."

"Sold," said Mateo.

"Sold, what?" asked Simone. There was another clunk from the hall and Simone went to open the door again.

"You're hired," said Mateo.

"What?" asked Simone, blinking at Mateo.

"Gabe, say hello to your new co-worker. Simone is going to help out during the event."

"Oh, thank God," exclaimed the boy, turning around the dolly to look at Simone and Mateo. "Hey, boss. Hey Simone. Wait until I put this down, and then I'll shake your hand." Gabe unloaded the fresh batch of wine crates next to the first one. Then wiped his hands on his jeans and offered Simone a hand to shake. "Gabe Gonzales. Nice to meet you."

"Nice to meet you too," said Simone, feeling like she had completely lost control of the situation.

"Oh, there you are," said Caleb, returning to the room. "Mateo Amante, please meet Simone Laurent if you haven't already."

"Hi, Caleb," said Mateo. "I did meet her, and I have, in fact, just decided to hire your prize show pony."

"That's show *poodle*!" exclaimed Caleb, glaring at Simone.

"Best in breed?" suggested Gabe with a grin.

"Exactly," replied Caleb.

"You might have mentioned that you were the owner," said Simone to Mateo, blushing.

"That would take all the fun out of everything," said Mateo, with a grandfatherly twinkle in his eye.

"So what's Simone going to be doing?" asked Gabe, looking at the group.

"Whatever anyone needs me to do, I guess," said Simone.

"We'll use her as an extra set of hands at the event, and she has marketing skills, so we'll turn her loose on the social media."

"Great," said Gabe, turning to Simone with a relieved look. "They keep expecting me to know what I'm doing because I'm under forty, but all I really know how to do is post stuff."

"Oh," said Simone, suddenly feeling like the situation had become three times more intense than it had been a few minutes ago and wondering where she'd buried all her resources on social media in her computer. On the other hand, she had gotten an *A* in that class, and she did have two thousand followers on Instagram, so it wasn't like she was a complete newb.

"Well, I'm pretty good at social media. And I can take some photos too. What's the core marketing message you're trying to express?" There was silence from everyone. "OK," said Simone, slowly, realizing that no matter what her grade had been, she was still light years ahead of the rest of the room. "Well, I guess I will be working on crafting that then."

"Paying off already," said Mateo, and Caleb chuckled.

"Well, it seems my mental rolodex has triumphed once again," said Caleb. "Simone, I believe I leave you in good hands. Give me a call when you're done here, and I'll pop up and get you."

"Oh, I'm sure someone can give her a ride home," said Mateo. "Maybe we can talk Jordan into it."

"Seems like it shouldn't be that hard," agreed Caleb, flexing his eyebrows at Mateo in a mysterious wiggle of conspiracy that Simone couldn't interpret.

"Indeed," agreed Mateo.

"I can do it," offered Gabe.

"I don't know about that," said Simone. "I hear that you tend to run into things."

Mateo laughed. "Shot down by your own mouth," he said. "Don't worry, Simone, we'll find you someone who knows how to drive."

Jordan

Jordan lifted the pH strip from the wine sample. He didn't need it to tell him what his taste buds had already confirmed the wine needed another few months in the cask, but he liked having the scientific verification. He noted the results on his laptop and prepared to move on to the next cask.

"Hey," said George, coming into the production warehouse from outside.

"Hey," said Jordan, making a final note.

"I thought you said last night we couldn't hire anyone?"

"Yeah, I did," said Jordan, concentrating on not overfilling his sample tube. "Mateo's been adamant."

"But Gabe just said we hired someone," said George.

Jordan looked up in surprise, and wine splashed over his hand. He hurried to shut the wine off and grabbed a towel. "What do you mean we hired someone?" he asked when he was finally not covered in wine.

"I don't know. I figured you would know," said George.

"Mateo didn't even say he was interviewing!"

"I don't know, man. I'm just telling you what I heard."

"Yeah, OK. I guess I'll ask him about it," said Jordan, surprised at his anger.

"Well, let me know what you find out. I'm going out to the far field. I'll be back around lunch. Shoot me a text when you know something."

"Yeah, OK," said Jordan.

After George was gone, Jordan pulled out his cell phone and dialed Mateo, but the call went straight to voice mail. Odds were Mateo didn't have it on him. While Jordan was considering what to do next, his phone rang in his hand, and he jumped in surprise.

"Hey Michelle," he said, picking up.

"Hey," said Michelle, without preamble. "Do you think you'd be willing to help me out with some unpaid labor?"

"Yeah, sure," said Jordan. "Whatever you need. Mateo hired someone."

"What?"

"He hired someone!"

"You sound mad," said Michelle. "But haven't you been on him for months to hire someone?"

"Yes, I have. And he keeps shooting me down. He said when I took over management duties I'd have decisions on staff. But today, he just went and hired someone without even letting me know."

Michelle sighed. "I really think you should have gone to that big winery out in Wenatchee."

"I don't like Wenatchee. I like it here. I like being able to see you and Graham and the kids whenever I want. I like Amante, and I even like Mateo. I mean, not right this second, but in general. But I feel like while he says I'm in charge, he keeps second-guessing everything I do."

"That's what I'm saying. You would have had an easier transition if you'd gone someplace where they didn't remember when you were twelve."

"Maybe I would have," said Jordan. "But I'm here now, and I'm really," he clenched his hand into an angry fist, "upset," he finished anticlimactically, and Michelle laughed.

"Sorry, it's not funny, but you sounded just like Mom then. If I were in the room, I'd be running to avoid having a wooden spoon flung at my head."

"She's a dead-eye," agreed Jordan. "And I'm about to start flinging beakers around, and they're a lot more breakable than wooden spoons."

"You've got to talk to Mateo. This kind of thing has got to stop. You need to be very clear about your boundaries."

"You know what? You're right. I've been putting it off because I keep thinking everyone will settle down and get used to it. But that's obviously not happening. I need to go talk to him. God even knows what kind of idiot he's hired."

"You are a valuable employee who needs to be respected," said Michelle.

"You need to stop reading those business books," said Jordan. "That's not a good pep talk."

Michelle laughed. "No? Hmm… What would my husband say?" Michelle cleared her throat and lowered her voice. "All right, team, we're down by seven, and we've got a minute and a half of play left, but you got this. You are the best on the court, and that is your ball! Now go get it!"

Jordan laughed. "Thanks, Michelle."

"Any time, baby brother. See you tonight."

Jordan hung up, went to the phone next to the door, and dialed the front office.

"Hey there," said a cheerful voice.

"Hey, Laureen," said Jordan. "Is Mateo with you?"

"Nope, I think he was showing the new hire around. Did you know we were hiring someone?"

"No, I didn't," said Jordan sourly.

"Hm. Well, I think they were going to do a quick tour and then look at the main courtyard for the event layout. Then they were going to end up back here, so I can finish up all the hiring paperwork. You can probably catch him if you head up here in a minute or two. Or I can tell him to call you."

"I'll come up," said Jordan.

Jordan supposed he shouldn't be as mad as he was—they really did need the extra person—but the more he thought about it, the more annoyed he became. He headed up to the office, taking the shortcut through the loading bay to get to the backside of the winery and the office area.

Jordan angrily slammed open the door to the interior courtyard, determined to find Mateo and put his foot down once and for all. He was tired of being second-guessed and having everything overturned on a whim. He crossed the threshold and took a few steps across the warm gray flagstones before coming to an abrupt halt.

There was a girl in the courtyard.

She was standing under the archway that led out to the fields. She had a tumble of long black hair that fell in soft waves down the back of her blue dress. He could only see a sliver of her profile, but her shape was perfection. As he watched, she lifted a graceful hand to caress a clump of dusky purple grapes dangling from the arbor over her head. She gently pulled the grapes down to her face and smelled the fruit. He knew what she was smelling—the earthy hint in the leaves, the tart overtures of the fruit, the bright sap of the vines, all mingling together into the scent he thought of as the birth of wine. It was the smell that first told him when the grapes were ready. For him, it was always the most personal moment of wine-making. The intimate moment of taking in the grapes with all his senses. And as he watched, this girl did the same thing. He loved the soft way she cradled them in her hands and held them to her face as if taking in every aspect with her whole being. She took his breath away.

"Oh, Jordan," said Mateo, coming out of the office on the far side of the courtyard. "Come meet Simone."

"Simone," stuttered Jordan, looking at his palm where the black scrawl of a phone number and name could still be read despite repeated washings. Then he looked up at the girl who had turned to face him. The softness had gone from her frame, and she was standing with her arms folded across her chest.

"Simone is going to be helping during the event," said Mateo, crossing the courtyard toward Jordan and beckoning to Simone. "She'll be doing some marketing work and general, all-around helping."

"Oh," said Jordan, going unwillingly to meet the pair in the center of the space near the fountain. He looked down and met Simone's frosty hazel gaze.

"Do you know anything about wine?" he asked, feeling defensive.

"I know about marketing," said Simone. "I was assuming *you* would know about wine, but perhaps I shouldn't be too swift in making assumptions."

"Jordan is our enologist," said Mateo, looking startled at Simone's tone.

"Not a mechanic, then?" asked Simone, raising her eyebrows.

"I never said I was a mechanic," said Jordan.

"You certainly didn't behave like a very good one," said Simone. "So I suppose I should have known."

"You can't have a dog in a garage!" snapped Jordan.

"I thought Skipper was nice," said Mateo, still confused. "I thought he could come up to the winery."

"I'm not having a dog in the Production Warehouse," said Jordan, trying to cling to some semblance of control.

"Well, of course not. But the office is fine," said Mateo.

"Some people like dogs," said Simone, her chin rising arrogantly.

"I like dogs! This is not... It's not... You're not supposed to be here!"

"Jordan!" said Mateo, sounding shocked. Simone's eyes went wide, and her arms adjusted from folded to wrapped around herself. She looked hurt and Jordan wished he could stuff the words back in his mouth.

"I'm sorry," said Jordan. "That didn't come out right."

"There was a better way?" asked Mateo, glaring at him.

"I just meant that I am surprised that she's here. I did not realize we were hiring anyone," he said, glaring back at Mateo, "and if we were, I thought I would be involved in the hiring process."

"It's only temporary," said Simone, quietly. "Until I pay for the motorhome repairs."

And now he felt like the biggest jerk in the universe.

"Welcome aboard," he said tightly. "We can use the help."

Then he turned on his heel and left before he could blurt out something else that would be a contender for the top ten stupidest statements ever.

PART 2:

A Romantic...
French Bordeaux

We recommend pairing this section with a Bordeaux. These wines are a symphony of citrus and floral notes, with a depth that mirrors the richness of a blossoming romance in spring. Like the tender beginnings of a new relationship, each sip reveals more with time. Bordeaux also employs the French *sur lie* process, a key touchstone in Jordan and Simone's journey.

Our Bordeaux pick, the *2020 Luminesce from L'Ecole and Estate Seven Hills Vineyard.*

TASTING NOTES: On the palate, fresh and crisp peach, canary melon, and lemon tart pervade, with fine notes of exotic jasmine, building to a persistent, tangy finish.

CHAPTER 4
Recovery

Simone

The sun was lowering in the sky, and the chill fall wind had blown in with a gust. Simone hugged her laptop to her chest and hurried up the back walkway to Sir Barkington's, following the little puddles of warmth from the path lights along the edge. She couldn't remember the last time she'd left Skipper alone for so long. What if he was panicking without her? She pushed open the kitchen door and stood panting on the threshold, taking in the scene.

Caleb, in a bright red apron, was holding out a tiny bit of bacon to Skipper, who was sitting next to the stove on a tall stool.

"What is this?" demanded Simone, waving at the cooking arrangement. "Cooking with Skipper?"

"He's an excellent assistant," said Caleb with a cheerful smile.

On the floor, Sir Barkington woke up and tried to sit up but banged his head into the lowest rung on the stool.

"Sir Barkington is in charge of cleaning up any spills," said Caleb.

"You didn't miss me at all, did you, you traitor?" Simone asked, putting her things down on the table.

Skipper finished his bacon treat and hopped off the stool, running to her with a happily wagging tail. Simone gathered him up in her arms and hugged him tight. "At least someone likes me."

"Now that doesn't sound like happy first-day commentary," said Caleb, crumbling the rest of his bacon over a casserole pan.

"What happened? No, wait, don't speak. There is wine open on the table. I was letting it breathe but wandered off. Pour us some, and then give me all the gory details."

Simone put Skipper down and reached for the bottle, wrinkling her nose when she saw it was an Amante Chianti Classico.

"The details aren't gory," said Simone, pouring the wine into glasses. "Only it turns out that Jordan Ryan was the mechanic who yelled at me yesterday, and when he saw it was me and Mateo said I was hired, Jordan said I didn't belong there."

Caleb paused, mouth agape, seemingly flummoxed by Simone's story.

"I'm sorry. I'm either going to need to hear that again or drink some wine so it makes sense."

Simone handed him a glass of wine, and Caleb laughed.

"I think I would prefer to do both now that I'm considering it. Go over it again. What happened? You seemed excited when I left."

"I was! I am! They need so much help, but it's all stuff that I know how to do! I really think I can actually help them, and that feels great. I was worried that Mateo was just... being nice, you know? I'm excited to be able to be doing what I went to school for. Even if it's short-term. And it would be experience to put on a resume. And then I turned around, and it was sweaty mechanic guy. Only he's not a mechanic. He's Jordan Ryan. Who everyone loves. I heard nothing but *oh, you should meet Jordan, Jordan's the best* from everyone I met at the winery. And then I meet Jordan, and he already hates me, and he said I didn't belong there."

Caleb sipped his wine with a frown. "That sounds entirely out of character for Jordan."

"It's a direct quote," said Simone, taking another drink. "And the worst part is that I really like this wine."

Caleb laughed. "He's brilliant at making wine. But apparently not brilliant at making friends, though."

"I don't know what happened," said Simone, sitting down. "Mateo apologized and said he would talk to Jordan, but I'm not sure it matters. How am I supposed to work there if Jordan hates me?"

"You are excited about this job, and you need the money," said Caleb sensibly. "You can't let him scare you away."

"That's true," said Simone, raising her chin. "He doesn't get to tell me where to work. I can do this job."

"That's right!" affirmed Caleb.

"And I can be great at it!"

"Preach it," agreed Caleb.

"So I am going to go back up there in the morning—"

"After you walk the dogs."

"After I walk the dogs. And I am going to show him that I do belong there because I am going to improve their social media presence, I'm going to update their website, and I am going to take such pretty pictures of his stupid wine that people will want to drink it off their screens."

"That's the spirit," said Caleb. "Now the dog treats are baking. What do you think about ordering pizza?"

"Sounds fabulous," said Simone. "Because I am starting tonight. I've got all their passwords, and I'm going to knock their socks off."

"I will get more wine," said Caleb.

Jordan

"Uncle Jordan! Uncle Jordan!" Mason sprinted down the walk toward Jordan, and Jordan switched the bottle of wine to his other hand so he could scoop up the seven-year-old. Mason was a happy-go-lucky blond kid with freckles and a hatred for the sunscreen his mother kept trying to slather over them. "Uncle Jordan! You need to tell Mom she's wrong!"

"You got it, bud," agreed Jordan instantly. Michelle appeared in the open doorway in her post-work outfit of jogging shorts and trainers.

"Mason, stop leaving the door open!"

"You're wrong!" bellowed Jordan.

"No, we get flies," said Michelle, looking puzzled. "Graham hates it."

Jordan laughed. "I just promised Mason I'd say you were wrong."

Michelle groaned and rolled her eyes. "Pumpkin loaf, I'm not wrong. I know you don't want me to be right, but the fact is that oil and gas are made from dead dinosaurs and other organic matter."

"I'm never riding in the car again!" wailed Mason. "You killed the brachiosaur!"

"I didn't kill anything! They were already dead! It's like the compost heap only really compressed."

"I'm not sure that's quite how that works," said Jordan.

"Close enough," said Michelle. "The key point here is that I'm not responsible for dead dinosaurs."

"Well, that's true," said Jordan.

"Uncle Jordan!" exclaimed Mason, looking betrayed.

"Sorry, bud. I'll back you on the broccoli, but not the brachiosaur."

Mason shook his head and wriggled out of Jordan's grasp onto the floor. "I am going to play horse without you," he said with an air of injured dignity and stalked past his mother with his nose in the air.

"That'll show *you*," said Michelle to Jordan, smothering a laugh. "Come on in."

"Thanks," said Jordan.

"Hey," Graham said, waving tongs at Jordan as they entered the kitchen. "I'm about to do manly grilling things. Grab a beer! Unless you brought wine?" He ended on a hopeful note.

Graham was a six-foot-three lanky guy with a sprinkle of gray in his beard and hair. He was a good teacher and a great basketball coach with a natural un-forced coach's enthusiasm. He also was a closet wine aficionado and Michelle had spent their first year of dating sponging off Jordan's wine knowledge before copping to the fact that she liked beer better. After a decade of marriage, they settled into his and hers beverage fridges in the basement.

"I did," said Jordan, hoisting the bottle.

"My man. Pop her open while I get these on the grill!"

Graham took his platter of undefined meats covered in sauce out to the back patio while Jordan scrounged for a wine opener.

"How did it go at work?" asked Michelle, twisting the top off a beer and taking a quick look in the oven at her roasting vegetables.

Jordan stopped mid-turn on the corkscrew with a sigh.

"That good?" asked Michelle with a laugh. "What happened?"

"You remember Simone?" asked Jordan.

"The girl you were a complete jerk to? Yeah," said Michelle. "I remember. Turns out she doesn't have the cash to fix the motorhome, by the way, so she was out job hunting today. Let me know if you know anyone who needs help during the festival."

"She got a job," said Jordan.

"That's great! She seemed sweet. Where at?"

"The winery," said Jordan gloomily.

"Oh no! She's the one who got hired?" exclaimed Michelle.

"Yeah, and after I talked to you I went storming up to the

office to talk to Mateo."

"Oh dear," said Michelle. "I'm not sure I like where this is going."

"I told her she wasn't supposed to be here," said Jordan.

"Jordan! Why would you say that?"

"I don't know! I was mad at Mateo; she was giving me the stink-eye, and I just meant... I don't know what I meant, but that's what came out, and then she looked really hurt."

"Jordan!"

"I know! I know! I'm a horrible person!"

"Well, did you apologize?"

"I tried to take it back and said we could use the help and turned tail and ran before I could say something else."

Michelle laughed.

"Michelle! It's not funny. I feel like such a jerk. I don't know what I'm supposed to do."

"Well, start with apologizing to her," said Michelle.

"What am I even supposed to say?" demanded Jordan, grabbing glasses from the cupboard.

"Say what to who?" asked Graham, coming back in.

"My genius baby brother managed to insult the pretty new girl who's working at the winery."

"Smooth move," said Graham, shoving an entire slice of cheese in his mouth.

"I'm using those," said Michelle, smacking at his hand.

"Youalwayscutextra," mumbled Graham, through the cheese.

"Don't talk with your mouth full, Dad," said nine-year-old Robin, coming into the kitchen with a book in one hand. Her sandy hair was close to Jordan's in color, but she had her father's tall frame.

"Is that a new library book?" asked Michelle.

"Yes?"

"No more library fines!" exclaimed Michelle.

"It's from the school library," said Robin. "I don't get fines there."

"Not all books are your books," said Michelle. "You have to give them back."

"I give them back," protested Robin.

"Eventually," added Graham, which made Jordan chuckle.

"You two are not helping," said Michelle sternly.

"Hey, Robin," said Jordan. "Go check my jacket pocket. I think there might be an Amazon card in it for you."

Robin squealed and ran to the hall.

"It's like ten bucks," said Jordan to Michelle's skeptical expression.

"I worry that someday she's going to end up in a house with nothing but books in it," said Michelle. "Wandering around in stretched-out cardigans and leaving empty tea cups everywhere."

"I think that's just called being a librarian," said Graham, accepting a glass of wine from Jordan. "And I believe that many of them live highly productive, almost normal lives."

Michelle, mid-sip, almost choked on a laugh. "Well, if she actually had a library of her own, you know, someplace else, I'd be happier. I didn't sign up for my house to be a library. I'm tired of tripping over books. And if I step on one more dinosaur, I'm going to start chucking them out the window."

"The triceratops is a menace to bare feet everywhere," agreed Graham. "But didn't you buy him the plesiosaur last week?"

"It was so cute!" complained Michelle. "And he wanted it so bad! Also, Jordan, you can't go around being mean to Simone. You have to go in tomorrow and apologize."

"How did we get from the plesiosaur to me and Simone?"

"You got tossed into the mom loop," said Graham. "Give her five minutes, and she'll complain about your laundry."

"I do my own laundry," said Jordan.

"Great," said Michelle. "Then you know how to clean up messes. Tomorrow, you'll just go up to her and say you're sorry."

"Michelle, I'm not seven."

"I didn't say you were!" Michelle looked offended. Jordan glanced at Graham, who gave him a tiny headshake that said it wasn't worth the argument.

Mason opened the door from the backyard. "Uncle Jordan, aren't you coming out to play horse?"

"I thought you were playing without me."

"You can't play horse by yourself," said Mason, looking like he thought Jordan was being ridiculous.

"He's got you there," said Graham.

"I don't know what I was thinking," said Jordan. "OK, but just one game because your mom wants to tell me how to run my life some more."

"Well," said Mason, nodding sagely, "she knows about stuff."

"I *do* know about stuff," said Michelle.

"Yeah," agreed Mason sincerely, while Graham silently tried to hide his laughter by turning away. "I just said that."

"Well, thank you," said Michelle as Mason pulled Jordan toward the basketball hoop. "Jordan! Shut the door!"

It wasn't until after dinner that he got any further uninterrupted adult time. Graham was cleaning the grill and Michelle had chased the kids upstairs to start the bedtime routines. Jordan sank into the fat cushions of a patio chair and enjoyed the sunset.

"Did you really insult some girl at work?" asked Graham.

"She's just temporary help for the Classic. She's trying to get money together to pay for the repairs on her motorhome," said Jordan. "But yeah, I really was a jerk. I don't know if I should just avoid her from now until the end of the event or try and actually say something. I feel bad."

"If you really feel that way, then say something," said Graham. "Say it for yourself, so you know you tried your best. The game's not over just because you flubbed a shot. It's never too late to make a comeback."

"You really are better at pep talks than Michelle," said Jordan, chuckling.

"She's more of a general than a coach," said Graham. "She'll get you to charge the enemy, but mostly because you want her behind you rather than in front of you."

Jordan laughed harder.

"What's so funny?" asked Michelle, coming back out to the patio.

"Nothing," said Graham. "How're the troops?"

"Brushing their teeth," said Michelle, dropping into the seat nearest the grill with an exhausted sigh. "You know, those two may be the death of me, but man, do we produce cute kids."

"Nailed it," agreed Graham, holding out his fist. Michelle promptly fist-bumped him.

Jordan laughed at their self-congratulations.

"You know," said Michelle, focusing on Jordan, "I've been thinking about Simone."

Jordan groaned. "Jeez, you're worse than Mom. I'm apologizing, OK?"

"Yeah, I figured you would. No, I was thinking about what you said about her being a tourist hipster. I don't think she is. She was really sweet and determined to pay the whole bill, even when I offered to knock a couple of bucks off. I think you should give her another chance."

"I think at this point," said Jordan, "we'll be lucky if she gives *me* another chance."

Simone

"And I have to spit it out?" asked Simone as she picked up the next glass. George laughed as he re-stoppered the bottle and put it back behind the bar in the tasting room. The tasting room wouldn't open for another hour, so they had the place to themselves.

"You don't have to, but you've got three more to go, and unless you want to be tipsy before noon, you probably should."

Simone sighed sadly. "Well, all right, but it seems like a waste."

Simone had spent the morning with Caleb, walking and feeding his doggy babysitting charges before coming up to the winery where, so far, she was experiencing the best working day of her life. Everyone had already noticed her efforts on the social media pages and had been incredibly complimentary. She had been allowed to bring Skipper almost everywhere and take all the photos she wanted, and now George insisted that she drink delicious wine. The only sad part was that he also insisted she spit it out.

George was attempting to train her to taste wine so that she could educate others and help with the larger crowds when the event happened. So far, she felt a bit silly, but she inhaled a sip, attempting to bring in air with it. Then swished it around her mouth, trying to bring it to the various parts of her tongue as George had instructed. Reluctantly, she spit the wine back into the spittoon that George had provided. It wasn't really a spittoon, but she'd already forgotten the proper wine-y name that George had called it.

"It was really smooth on the front of my tongue and then hit kind of a summer feeling," she tasted her mouth with her tongue, "I guess that's blackberry at the back," reported Simone. George beamed.

"Yes! Excellent. This is last year's summer Barbera."

"I got it right?"

"It's not a right or wrong answer," said George, laughing. "It's what you taste. Some people have more taste buds than others, and some people understand the taste buds they do have better. It's more about training yourself to identify and appreciate what's there. Although, you do seem to be finding the flavors easily. You're sure you haven't done this before?"

"I really haven't. We used to drink wine at home all the time, but no one made a thing about it. Except Grandpa. He was picky. I think we just always bought what he wanted. Although, I have to admit, now that I'm thinking of it, I haven't found a lot of wines I like since leaving home. A lot of stuff is sort of…" She made a blech face. "I don't know. It has that sort of—boom—in-your-face flavor and then that's it. There's none of the nice ahhhh afterwards. I probably should have taken more careful notes when Dad was buying stuff. But I thought wine was just wine."

George twitched all over as though she had electrocuted him. "I promise you that it is not," he said fervently.

"Sorry," said Simone, laughing. "I didn't know. I must have gotten spoiled by all of Grandpa's wine. He taught Agricultural Science at the University of Colorado and could go on for hours about how the grapes in each wine were grown. He still had racks of it after he died. I don't think we bought wine for another four years. He also left labels on everything as to what year the bottles should be drunk."

"Now that is a nice thing to do for your loved ones," said George sincerely, looking impressed, and Simone chuckled.

"All right," he said, pouring out another small glass, "let's see what you think about this one and if it would be Grandpa approved. Jordan has a whole theory on the terroir on this blend, but we'll see what you taste."

"Terroir?"

"That's the entire natural environment that produces the grapes. Soil, sunshine, elevation, topography. Everything. That's what your grandfather was lecturing you about."

"This is so fascinating! Hold on." Simone paused to make some notes. She felt like she ought to be recording everyone she encountered. They all dropped quote-worthy statements left and right. She was having a hard time keeping up. She paused and jotted down another idea. The winery offered so many opportunities for creating content. She was going to have to make a media calendar.

Her only worry was that she had yet to see Jordan. That thought gave her nervous butterflies in her stomach, but she hoped she could avoid him entirely if she just went back to her tiny cubbyhole of an office. That probably wasn't a long-term solution, but she hoped to make it at least through the afternoon.

Jordan

"Holy cow," said Gabe, dropping the mail on Jordan's desk. "Have you seen any of our social media pages?"

"What? Why?" Jordan had been focused on the outputs from the latest grape delivery and had to replay Gabe's words in his head to make them make sense.

"Seriously, I don't know if that new Simone chick stayed up all night or if she's just that good, but everything looks killer! She's got buy links, message buttons, new photos, and all sorts of stuff. I can't believe it! I actually shared this morning's post on my own feed."

"You weren't sharing it before?" asked Jordan, frowning.

"No. We posted lame stuff," said Gabe.

"You were posting it!"

"Yeah, that's how I know it was lame. But this Simone girl somehow waved a magic wand and now we look all cool and stuff. I didn't know that the Classic was that big of a deal. Her post on the history of the event this morning made us sound like we're cool for even getting invited, let alone hosting."

"It's a prestigious event!" said Jordan. "We campaigned for three years to be hosts. How were you not getting this before?"

"I don't know," said Gabe with a shrug. "Anyway, you should check out all the pages. They look awesome."

Gabe continued on his rounds as Jordan flipped open the internet on his desktop. Gabe hadn't been kidding. The winery's social media pages had all been revamped, streamlined and looked twice as good. He couldn't even put his finger on what she'd done, but everything looked more professional. He read the morning's post and scratched his head. They sounded more professional, too, and she had links and hashtags to the Classic's social media pages. It was everything Jordan had wanted but lacked the skills to do. He'd only been able to point and say *not good* without being able to articulate how to do better. Simone might hate him, but she was obviously good at her job. Now he looked like an even bigger jerk than before.

Jordan scrubbed his hand through his hair and took a deep breath. He could do this. Coming to a decision, he stood up and headed for the main office.

Laureen wasn't at the front desk, so he went further into the nest of offices. The main building had been converted sometime in the fifties to accommodate office staff, and everything had the ad hoc non-OSHA-approved feeling of an on-the-fly conversion. He liked it, but he was sure that Mateo longed to have everything brought up to code.

Jordan thought they'd stashed Simone in the tiny back room next to the supply closet, which was probably bigger than her office. He headed in that direction, but before he got to Simone's office, he heard a small shriek.

"Um... help?" called a voice.

He hurried forward a few steps and looked through the doorway into the supply room and saw Simone trying to hold up a large box of pens that was threatening to spill off a top shelf onto her head and bring down three other boxes with it.

"Hold on!" He reached around her to push the pens back up on the shelf.

"I just wanted one!" said Simone, turning around, and then he realized he was within hugging proximity. He took a rapid step back, tripped over something, and sat down heavily on the box of copy paper.

Simone made a little squeak and grabbed for him. "No, I'm OK," he said flailing around, trying to recover his dignity and balance without success at either. She grabbed his forearm, pulling him back upright, and Jordan found himself back where he started—way too close. "I'm OK," he said again, staring down into her hazel eyes.

"Sorry!" she said. "I didn't mean to—"

"That was my fault," he said. "Ought to look where I'm going."

"Sorry," she said again, breathlessly. She looked worried.

"Um," he said. Now that he was here, he couldn't remember any of the carefully worded statements he'd been composing on the way over. "Hi. I wanted to, um... The social media pages look great."

"Thanks," she said, but still looked worried.

"I'm sorry about yesterday. I shouldn't have said that. That wasn't about you. I lost my temper about something else. I was a jerk." The words flowed out without any planning, and he felt relieved to have them out in the open, even if they weren't poetry.

"I want to do a good job," she said earnestly. "I think I can help. I'm not trying to be somewhere I'm not."

"I think you're helping already," he said.

"Really?" she asked, smiling shyly, brushing a lock of hair behind her ear.

"All the stuff you've done already is great. I can't imagine what you'll manage to accomplish on day two."

"Well, I do have some ideas," she said. "And I had this great one for social media this morning. George gave me tasting training."

"Oh, that's good," he said, nodding although he was barely listening. It was just that her lips looked so good when she talked.

"But I thought maybe… I mean, George said that you were the one I should talk to for quotes about the wine."

"Quotes about the wine?" repeated Jordan, trying to pay attention to what she was saying.

"Well, I want to do a famous quotes series about wine on social media and intersperse it with quotes from us—I mean, the winery—about the philosophy behind the wines."

"Oh," said Jordan. "Um. That's kind of a big conversation. I'm not sure I can squeeze it down to social media size."

"No, that's my job," said Simone. "I do all the squeezing."

"I don't think squeezing is allowed during working hours," said Laureen's amused voice from the door of the office supply room. Laureen was a fifty-something grandmother of three. She had seen everything and periodically liked to remind people of it.

Simone blushed bright red and looked from Laureen to Jordan in horror. She took the same awkward step Jordan had earlier and almost pitched backward into the copy paper. Jordan caught her arm and pulled her upright.

"We were talking about squeezing quotes down to social media size," said Jordan.

"Uh-huh," said Laureen. "Simone, honey, I've got lunch in the break room whenever you're ready."

"We can talk about wine philosophy later," said Jordan, smiling down at Simone.

"OK," said Simone. "I'll see you later." She hurried out the door, still looking pink. And adorable. Laureen raised an eyebrow at him but didn't say anything before following Simone to the break room.

Jordan left the office supply closet, trying not to smile. He felt one hundred percent better about Simone.

Caleb watched as Simone checked her hair in the hall mirror for the fifth time that morning.

"Big day today?" he asked.

"We're starting to set up for the Classic in the town square. I don't know what I'm doing exactly. But I'm excited to see it start to come together."

"Is everyone going to be there?" asked Caleb, probing for what had put Simone all a-twitter.

"Well, no. Just Mateo and me, um, Jordan."

"That's right, you said Jordan apologized?" He put down Sir Barkington's dog dish with one of the homemade dog treats on top.

"Yes," said Simone, a flush creeping onto her face. "He said he was mad about something else and had been a jerk and he saved me from dumping pens on my head."

"The gentlemanly thing to do," said Caleb, feeling suspicious of his new friend's pink cheeks.

"Jordan said he really liked what I'd done with their social media, too," said Simone, turning back to the mirror. "I guess I was wrong about him. I think working at the winery is going to be great. I just need my aunt to send me some money, and everything will be perfect. I'll be able to get my life back on track."

"It certainly seems that way," said Caleb.

"I can feel it," said Simone confidently. "I know, I know. There's no such thing as luck or fate. I should probably stop being silly. But I can't help feeling like everything is going my way for once. And now that Jordan doesn't hate me, I don't see what could go wrong."

"Neither do I," agreed Caleb. "But you know that not going to plan and going wrong are two different things, right? Sometimes life is all about the happy accidents."

"Thank you, Bob Ross," said Simone with a laugh.

"A man ahead of his time. But sadly, not ahead of his perm."

"That was a perm?" gasped Simone.

"What did you think it was?" asked Caleb.

"I don't know! Just his hair! I never questioned it. I learned how to draw mountains from him!"

"I don't think his perm impacts that," said Caleb.

"Well, yes, but I'm just so shocked. I'm not sure how to process this information."

"I'm sure you'll recover," said Caleb, chuckling. There was a sharp honk from a car horn out front.

"Laureen's here," said Simone. "OK, wish me luck and I'll do the second walk with Marmaduke when I get home, so don't worry about that."

"I will count on it," said Caleb, and Simone ran out the front door and down the stairs with Skipper at her heels.

"Well, Sir Barkington," said Caleb to his basset hound, who was lounging on the low-slung dog couch by the back door, "I do believe that our new friend has a crush on Jordan Ryan. I wonder if I shouldn't toddle around to Ryan's Garage and see if Michelle has any insight into how Jordan feels on the subject?"

Sir Barkington extended one paw off the couch as if contemplating getting up for breakfast but not quite committing.

"Yes," agreed Caleb, "I know how you feel."

Caleb had just decided to put off the visit to the garage until later when there was a knock on the front door. Sir Barkington roused himself enough to let out a single woof.

"Excellent effort, dear boy," said Caleb and went to open the door.

On the front porch was a chic older woman who looked oddly familiar.

"Hello," she said, taking off her sunglasses, revealing hazel eyes that were strikingly similar to Simone's. "Are you Caleb Bennett? I'm Juliette Laurent. I'm Simone's aunt."

CHAPTER 5
Setting Up

Simone

"So what am I supposed to be doing?" asked Simone anxiously. She and Jordan were standing in the town square next to a fountain that looked similar to the one on the edge of town. The square served as a public park and had an old-world charm to it. The fountain wasn't as fancy as the one at the edge of town—just a tall fluted vase shape spilling water into a broad base—but it seemed perfect for sitting and watching the world go by.

Luckless kept surprising her. She'd seen her fair share of small towns as she traveled across the country and she couldn't help feeling that this one was unusual—everyone genuinely seemed to care about making their town special. Most of the town's important buildings were on the square, from the town hall and library to the mansion turned museum of the town founder, Homer J. Price. She watched as the sun hit the bright brass finial on the top of the turret of the Price Mansion and lifted her camera to snap a picture. She knew it was fall, so the light was prone to being soft and mellow and perfect, but somehow, everything seemed to be a hazy romantic gold. All of her pictures were going to turn out looking magical.

She had Skipper's leash clipped to one of the belt loops on her shorts, her camera around her neck, and a backpack containing her notepad, work gloves, and a bottle of water. She thought she had covered all the contingencies. Jordan was wearing jeans and a button-up with the sleeves rolled up. He looked effortlessly easy—Simone tried to derail that train of thought but couldn't—

on the eyes.

"Well," said Jordan, "we're here to advise on the layout of the event so that we get the wineries placed optimally. The main judging will take place in the ballroom of Price Mansion." He pointed to the Victorian gingerbread of a house on one side of the square next to the library. "We have wineries coming in from Australia, Venezuela, France, Italy, and all over the US. We'll all do a special wine-tasting social each night of the event."

"Right," said Simone, whipping out her notepad and checking her chicken scratch writing. "Tickets are a hundred and fifty bucks a person!"

"Have you been taking notes?" asked Jordan, a laugh bubbling in his voice.

"Yes! I don't want to get anything wrong. And the wine from the tasting is paired with food from Washington restaurants, right? The menu's sounded to die for. Also, I got a call from someone this morning who was panicking about her shrimp delivery arriving early and wanted to know if we knew any local restaurants that would be willing to donate refrigerator space. I told her I'd check and call her back."

Jordan's eyes lifted skyward, appearing to think. "Call over to Basic Biscuits and see if they'd be willing to share a little room. They're partnering with us at the booth one of the days to do a raw honey and roasted goat cheese appetizer to go with our rosé."

"That does not sound like a basic biscuit," said Simone.

"Yeah, they pretty much do anything *but* a basic biscuit. The owner is excited to get her restaurant out in front of so many people, so we might be able to sweet-talk her into sharing her fridge if it's not a ton of space."

"Awesome," said Simone, jotting down a note. "I'll call everyone shortly. Thanks. OK, back to the layout. The judging and the fancy tastings are in the mansion, but the wineries and public tastings are all out here?"

"All the wineries that submit wine for judging will also have a booth to sell wine at and offer samples. So they have to be in the wine garden area and there has to be security to keep it over twenty-one. There will be wine-themed events outside the wine garden area. Grape stomping, bottle ring toss, and other general festival stuff. Linda Thornton," he pointed at Linda across the square, "is the event planner."

"Oh, I know Linda!" Simone waved, and Linda waved back. "She's nice."

"She's very nice," agreed Jordan. "She has a lot of the logistics figured out already, but there's stuff like port-a-potties, access to ice, and hand washing stations that she wants us to comment on before they get everything set. She has her opinions, of course, but she and the mayor don't quite see eye to eye on the placement."

"Well, the mayor can be pretty gung-ho," said Simone, and this time, Jordan actually did laugh.

"How long have you been in town?"

"Three whole days. But I heard all about the roadway improvements and the mayor on the first day," said Simone airily.

"Practically a native," said Jordan. "So basically, we're here to represent the wineries."

"And back up Linda against the mayor?" guessed Simone.

"That too," said Jordan. "As the primary sponsor of the event, we have a bit more clout."

"Awesome," said Simone. "OK, well, I think from a marketing standpoint, I want to catch some shots of any of the tents going up and start creating a narrative about the winery's support of the town."

"But we do support the town," said Jordan, sounding puzzled.

"Yes," said Simone. "I just said that."

"No, you said you were creating a narrative. It doesn't need to be created. We already do that."

"Oh," said Simone, realizing the problem. "Ah. Um, yes. You do. But that is not reflected in any of your marketing materials or online presence. You need to tell people you're doing it."

"That seems like bragging," said Jordan, looking uncomfortable.

"Maybe if you were a person, it would be," said Simone. "But it's a business. You want customers to feel like buying your wine isn't just good for them personally, but a good thing to do for others."

"It seems so calculating," said Jordan, frowning.

"It is a bit calculating," said Simone. "But think of it like dressing up for a date."

"What do you mean?"

"Well, you want your date to like you, so you put on nicer clothes than what you would wear on laundry night. That's calculating. But it's not lying. You want this person to like you because you like them. Well, the Amante Winery likes wine lovers and we want them to like us back, so we're going to put on our Sunday best and try to impress."

"I think that's the best explanation of marketing I've ever heard," said Jordan. "It also explains why it makes me uncomfortable—I never know what to wear on a date either."

Simone chuckled and refrained from suggesting he just go shirtless because that would impress any girl with a pulse. Then she wondered if he'd intentionally said that to let her know he was single. Not that it mattered because she was really just on her way to Colorado. But… a girl could daydream.

"Simone, honey!" exclaimed Linda, approaching them. Simone jumped, startled and a little embarrassed because she had been caught staring at Jordan. "And little Skipper!"

Linda bent down to pet Skipper before standing up to hug Simone. She had dressed up a bit for a work day in a plain blue blouse and black slacks, but she still radiated comfortable mom-type warmth.

"What are you doing with this big lug?" she asked, leaning over to hug Jordan.

"Hey Linda," said Jordan. "Simone's going to be working with us through the Classic. She's doing marketing and social media, so she will be taking pictures today."

"Fantastic!" exclaimed Linda, beaming at the two of them.

"That will be all right, won't it?" asked Simone. "I mean, with the mayor or the city and everyone?"

"Oh, good gravy, yes. I'm sure, Tricia, the mayor—Tricia Mc-Clavey—did I tell you about her? She's over there talking to Mateo and Rob, the head of the maintenance division."

Simone glanced at Jordan as Linda's flood of names and back-stories washed over her. He was grinning gleefully as if he knew very well that she wouldn't remember a tenth of the information.

"Anyway," concluded Linda, "long story short, I'm sure Tricia will be happy to have someone else talking about how fabulous the town is."

Simone glanced at Tricia, who had small-town big hair and a sensible pair of sneakers under her slacks and blazer. Tricia had the determined expression of someone who got things done.

"Well, I'll do my best," said Simone, feeling overwhelmed.

"Which is better than the entire rest of us put together," said Jordan with such confidence that she felt as though he might actually be right, and she stood up a little taller. It was nice to have someone who believed in her.

"Never underestimate a Luckless-ite," said Linda, cheerfully.

"Not quite," said Simone, smiling at Linda's inclusion of her among the town residents.

"Close enough," said Linda, not to be deterred. "Luckless by blood, anyway. Now, here come Tricia and Mateo. Simone, what do you think about going over there and taking some pictures? Then I'll be able to point out how horrible it would be if everyone taking pictures of the entrance was also taking pictures of the port-a-potties."

Simone laughed. "What, you don't think three yellow and black striped *Do Your Bees-ness* outhouses really scream wine event?"

"Funnily enough, no, I do not," said Linda.

"I'll go shake my head sadly at my camera," said Simone. "Find you in a bit?" she asked, turning to Jordan, and he nodded.

Simone went where Linda had indicated and stood around snapping what were sure to be lackluster photos while trying to keep an eye on the group by the fountain. Mateo had gone fully formal in slacks and a suit jacket. He looked every inch the affluent wine owner with a casual elegance to his style. It didn't hurt that he was tall and distinguished-looking. She wondered why he'd never been married. He seemed like a great guy.

Simone walked a few feet and then turned back to take a photo of Mateo with the Mayor. She felt like it would be a good one to have. They were framed by the Price Mansion, and the shot looked like a power shot for both of them. She couldn't wait to get it up on social media.

After a bit, Ron from maintenance stomped off, and Jordan turned and gave her a subtle thumbs up. Assuming she was now free to take the pictures she wanted, Simone moved on to a shot that she thought would be interesting. The arched sign that was to go over the entryway looked like it had great potential. She took one last look at Jordan who was nodding along to something Mateo was saying, but then he pointed across the square at something else. Both Linda and Mateo paused, looking thoughtful.

Simone smiled. She had met a lot of people in her travels and she had begun to recognize a few types of people. After only three days in Luckless, she had come to believe that Jordan was one of the quiet ones who did all the work and only got a tenth of the praise. Almost every time she asked a question at the winery, someone started their answer with *well, Jordan would know the most, but...*

She was pleased that at least Mateo and Linda seemed to recognize when to listen to him.

Juliette

Juliette stood in the town square and looked around in bemusement. One side of the square was the town hall, the next was the library, and the grand Price Mansion, the original home of the town founder. The other two sides were made up of the movie theater, still operating, and a mishmash of shops. The square itself, with the wide granite pavers, was the same, but everything else was different. The town hall had been completely rebuilt. The library, remodeled. The record store was gone. So was Madame Leona's Trends, where she had bought her prom dress. The movie theater had been restored to its art deco glory, and the barbershop had somehow been re-vintaged. Previously, it just looked like a crummy old barbershop from the fifties. Now, everything was a newer, shinier version of the different decades. It was what everyone wanted vintage to be—eclectic and cute— rather than what vintage usually was—left over from Grandad's closet. Even the Price Mansion had been covered in fresh paint. The entire town felt fresher. She remembered it being grungy and small. It was still petite, but somehow it was no longer shabby. Or maybe it was just refusing to be painted with the bitter brush of her memory.

Set up for the Decanter Classic was underway. White tents were springing up across the square, and little golf carts were busy ferrying supplies and equipment to-and-fro. She looked for Simone's dark head or Skipper's wagging tail. The delightful Caleb Bennett had been confident that she was here. But in her memory the square wasn't very big, so the task of finding Simone had seemed manageable. But her memories had not included so many people. If she were honest, her memory had mostly included one particular person and one particular rainy summer afternoon.

There was a fountain in the middle of the square—another donation from the Amante family, although it was much smaller than the one on the outskirts of town. Juliette approached it, feeling as if it were one of the few steady anchor points in a world that had changed while she wasn't looking. Only as she got closer did she realize that the man standing next to it was Mateo Amante.

She paused, her heart jack-hammering. His hair had gone silver, but it was still him. That arching nose and those broad shoulders—there was no mistaking Mateo. He was as handsome as ever. She stopped a few feet away, but he appeared lost in contemplation as the water trickled down into the basin of the fountain.

"Do you remember the day you walked me home from the library in the rain?" she asked, and he spun around, staring at her in astonishment.

She took off her hat and sunglasses, feeling embarrassed, suddenly wondering if he *would* remember. He took a step forward, reaching out, and then dropped his hand as if uncertain that an embrace would be welcome.

"I held my coat over our heads. You smelled like rose petals," he said.

"We got soaked," said Juliette.

"It was worth it," he said. They both paused and Juliette didn't know what to say next.

"Simone…" he began.

"She called me. She sounded excited about the job. I thought maybe it was time I came back."

"You said you'd never come back," he said, and Juliette winced.

"I was eighteen, Mateo. And I was hurt."

"I was twenty-one and stupid," he said. They paused again. She wondered what he was seeing when he looked at her. "Do you want to get dinner?" he asked.

"I'd love to. I'm staying at Sir Barkington's."

"I meant right now."

"It's barely lunchtime," said Juliette with a laugh.

"Lunch now, then dinner later," he said, smiling easily. "I know where there is some fantastic wine."

"I'm fairly confident it's at your house," said Juliette, raising an eyebrow. Mateo was handsome, and his family was wealthy—Juliette had always known he was confident, but she didn't remember him being quite so bold.

"Possibly true," he said, grinning sheepishly. "But there's a lot more to see. The town has changed so much."

"I can tell," said Juliette, looking around in distress. "I'm not sure I was ready for it to change."

"Some of the changes are good," he said and held out his hand. "I can show you everything you missed."

"Right now?" asked Juliette, laughing, but taking his hand.

"I think we've waited long enough," he said. "Don't you?"

"Yes," she said, the laughter dying away. "I think maybe so."

Jordan

Jordan tried to focus on what Linda was saying as he watched Simone chat with the maintenance crew putting up one of the tents. She got them to pose for a selfie, one of them holding up Skipper into the frame and then they all crowded around to see the photo on her phone, laughing.

Simone had been all over the square, talking to everyone, taking pictures, Skipper trotting at her heels. Skipper, he realized, was her secret weapon. Everyone wanted to talk to the cute terrier, and once they were petting the dog, she got them to agree to pictures. The notifications on his phone were blowing up as she posted the pics to Instagram. The hearts for each post were more than double what the winery had been getting for his occasional picture of grapes.

"She's such a good photographer," said Linda, glancing at her phone and then across the square at Simone. "I'm standing right here. I saw her take that photo. I did not think it would look that..." She paused, seeming to look for words.

"Cool?" suggested Jordan. "Scroll back further and you can see some shots she did of the fields yesterday. I'd frame any of those. I don't know how we got this lucky. She's exactly what we need."

"Hm," said Linda, eyeing him critically. "Are you sure she's not exactly what *you* need?"

"She's not staying," said Jordan. "She's only temporary."

"People can change their minds," said Linda. "Her family is from here. She could decide to stick around. Don't let that stop you from taking a chance."

"We're working together," said Jordan. "I don't have time to think about dating. And you, Linda Thornton, are a busybody."

"Yes," said Linda, "I am. And I also know your mother. She wants more grandbabies."

Jordan snorted. "Tell her to talk to Michelle. I have it on good authority that they make cute kids."

"Yes, they do," said Linda, with a laugh. "Now tell me what you think about the hand washing stations. Is that going to be enough, or should we add one more?"

Jordan was relieved that Linda let the subject drop. He didn't know what else to say. Simone was beautiful, talented, and the entire reason she was in his life was so that she could get out of it. What was the point of asking her out if she was only going to be gone in a week or two?

Jordan offered his opinions on hand washing stations and then went toward Simone. She was bent over, lining up a photo, while Skipper snapped at flies and looked bored. Jordan waved at the little dog, who immediately perked up, happy to have someone take an interest in him. Simone gave a yell as Skipper bolted toward Jordan, and Jordan lunged forward to catch her. But the sound of Simone in distress sent the little dog hurtling back toward his owner, looping both of them into the leash and slamming them together. Jordan wrapped his arms around Simone and tried to plant his feet against the juggernaut of a terrier.

"Oh!" said Simone, looking up at him, dazed.

Jordan was suddenly very aware that he was holding armfuls of Simone and all he could think was that every inch of her was magical, from her perfect hazel eyes to all the curves that were pressed up against him. The heat of the day brought the scent of her wafting up to him like the perfect bouquet on a wine, and he wanted to inhale and taste her. She smelled like lavender and honey. She would be the ideal pairing with goat cheese and a dry Riesling. He leaned down, tempted to plant a kiss on her mouth, but Skipper gave a sharp bark of disapproval from his tangled position behind Simone's legs.

"You smell good," Jordan blurted out and then felt himself immediately flush red.

"I shower," said Simone, blushing in turn.

Skipper barked again and tugged on the leash.

"Skipper," said Simone, looking down at him. "You are a bad dog. Let me see if I can…"

She tried to turn around to untangle the leash but only managed to rub her entire self all over Jordan. He thought if matters continued, he would need to stick his head—and other parts of him—in one of the ice stations. Finally, unable to take much more, he reached down, unclipped the leash from her shorts, and unwound Skipper from that end.

"Oh," said Simone, breathlessly. "That was a good idea. Thanks."

"No problem," said Jordan, concentrating on the leash and avoiding eye contact.

"Skipper, what's the rule?" demanded Simone. "Never ruin Mama's photos!"

"Does he follow that rule?" asked Jordan, handing over the leash.

"Mostly?" suggested Simone, looking like the answer was closer to *barely*.

They stared at each other and Jordan struggled to find a safe topic of conversation.

"It's almost lunchtime," he said. "I was going to find Mateo and grab some lunch before heading back up to the winery."

"Oh good," said Simone. She paused. "I need to go back to the winery today, too. I'm cracking open the website." She made a scared face. "Actually, I already looked at the back end yesterday. It's WordPress, so I think I should be able to figure it out, but web stuff always makes me nervous."

"I've done some updates," said Jordan, amazed that his mouth was carrying on a real conversation. "I might be able to help." His mouth was clearly the only functioning part of him because all he could think about was putting his arms back around Simone and doing all the things the rest of him wanted to do.

"Thanks," she said, then looked around the square. "Where is Mateo, by the way?" she asked, turning back to him.

"What?" he asked. His ears weren't fully operating either.

"Mateo? Where did he go?"

"I…" Jordan finally looked away from Simone and scanned the square. "I swear he was just over by the fountain a little bit ago."

His phone jangled with a text, and Jordan pulled out his phone and looked at the message.

"Or he's unexpectedly having lunch with someone else. Uh…"

That seemed unlike Mateo, but it was his prerogative. It wasn't like they'd had firm lunch plans.

"Well, I guess it's just you and me for lunch?" asked Simone with a smile.

"Yeah, I guess so," Jordan said, smiling back.

Simone

"Hey, Caleb!" chirped Simone coming in the back door, carrying her box of wine bottles.

"Well, hello," said Caleb, looking up from putting groceries away in the fridge. "What have you got there?"

"I have wine! I used my employee discount to get you wine

for next week."

"Well, that was sweet of you," said Caleb, looking as pleased as she had hoped he would.

"I bought what we drank the other night and then whatever Jordan told me to buy. I hope that's OK."

"I'm sure that it will be," said Caleb, tucking the celery away and turning around. "Did you find your aunt?"

"My aunt?" asked Simone, puzzled.

Caleb had changed into his afternoon attire, which always included a bow tie that matched Sir Barkington's. Today's was a dark navy with bright green dots over a blue cotton shirt. He looked dapper.

"She arrived a little after you left. I put her in the Paprika Room, and then she went down to the square to find you. I thought for sure you'd run into her there."

"No. I was there until almost one! And Jordan and I had lunch at a café right there." Simone pulled her phone out of her pocket and checked the messages. "She didn't call me."

"Hello!" called a voice from the front door.

"In here," yelled Caleb, which roused Sir Barkington enough to emit a half-hearted growl.

Juliette breezed into the kitchen, looking like a lifestyle shot that would be tagged *beautiful, mature woman*. She was wearing white linen and carried a straw sunhat and navy purse.

"Aunt Juliette!"

"Hello, darling! I've found you at last!"

"I didn't know you were looking!" exclaimed Simone, feeling guilty.

"Well," said Juliette, pausing to hug her, "I must admit that I wasn't looking that hard. I went to find you and then ran into some people and started reminiscing. You know how it is. Suddenly, half the afternoon is gone and how can you say *no* to dinner?"

Caleb laughed. "Juliette, I believe you are living *my* best life. Add in a glass of wine, and that's how I want it to be all the time."

Juliette chuckled. "Well, it's not half bad, I'll admit."

"But Aunt Juliette, what are you doing here?" asked Simone.

"Well, I thought I should come rescue you," said Juliette.

"I don't need rescuing," said Simone, sounding more clipped than she meant to.

"Well, that's what Caleb said," said Juliette, ignoring Simone's tone. "Which was why I didn't feel terribly guilty about not finding you this afternoon. But I also thought it was time I came back and had a look at the old place. I haven't been back since the family moved, you know. You don't mind terribly if I vacation while you pull yourself up by your bootstraps, do you?" Juliette's eyes twinkled, and Simone felt her momentary bad mood dissipate.

"No, of course not. It's good to see you! I just feel a bit bad that I'll be working and won't be able to hang out very much."

"I'm sure I can look up some old friends," said Juliette. "Don't worry. I'll just be happy to see more of you while we're here."

"That will be nice," said Simone, suddenly smiling.

And it *was* going to be nice. Simone liked her aunt and as much as she didn't want to be rescued, she did like that Juliette was willing to do it. And besides, Aunt Juliette was old. She would probably stick close to the house, play with the dogs, and be company for Caleb. It would be a nice, laid-back vacation for Juliette.

CHAPTER 6
Taking Risks

Jordan

Jordan tightened a bolt on the car and stepped back. He hoped he'd have her all put back together by the time the Classic was through. He was never planning on admitting it to anyone, but in his head, there was a perfect daydream about driving down the freeway with the Classic cup in the passenger seat and the wind in his hair. Although in the last day or two, the daydream had started to include Simone in the passenger seat and Skipper and the cup in the back.

The old barn on the Amante property had never been officially designated as his, but George had come through at some point and tacked up a wooden sign that read: JORDAN'S BAT CAVE. So he figured that made it official by Amante standards. He did all his best thinking in here—from how to fix the Spider to new ideas for wine. This was the place he could experiment without anyone looking over his shoulder. And at the moment, while his fingers were working on the car his brain was working overtime on Simone. What if Linda was right? What if he was missing out on something great because he was scared of taking a risk?

Yesterday's lunch had just been sandwiches and soda, but it had left him with all the buzzed feelings of an actual date. He'd driven Simone back up to the winery and then felt like a fool, leaving her at the office while fighting back the urge to kiss her on the cheek and ask if he could call on her again tomorrow. Laureen had given him the severe mom eye as he'd backpedaled his way out to the processing tanks.

"Jordan?"

Jordan stepped around the corner and saw Simone standing hesitantly in the doorway of the barn.

"Hi," she said, waving and then looking embarrassed, which was precious. "Um, I'm supposed to write some copy on the Barolo d'Amante for the Classic and Mateo said you should be the one to give me a tasting and tell me about it."

Jordan made a note to have a word with Mateo later. Mateo could just as easily have given Simone a tasting. This smacked of a setup. Was everyone trying to push him and Simone together?

"Yeah. Of course!" He turned to go into the workroom and then realized he was still holding a wrench and a greasy rag. "Give me just a sec," he said awkwardly, displaying the tool, before turning back toward the car. Simone followed him into the garage portion.

"Still no luck fixing it?" she asked.

"I'm close," said Jordan, and Simone nodded supportively but a shade too quickly. "You don't believe me, do you?"

"My dad used to say the same thing about the motorhome," she said, clearly suppressing a smile.

"That's right. Michelle said it had been retrofitted?" Jordan tucked the wrench away and swiped at the worst of the grease on his hands.

"Yeah, this road trip was his dream. He bought the motorhome my senior year of high school, but it took him all through my college years to get it fixed up. He wanted to see the U.S. He had all his routes mapped out and everything."

"Well, why didn't he come along?" asked Jordan. He looked up from his hands and realized he'd asked the wrong question. Simone looked stricken.

"Well, when he got sick, I promised I'd go with him," she said, then paused to clear her throat. Her eyes dropped to the floor. "And when we knew he wouldn't get better, I promised I'd take his ashes to all fifty states. This is the last stop."

"Oh," said Jordan, simultaneously wanting to hug her and realizing that every single one of his assumptions about Simone had been wrong.

"I'm really sorry," he said. "That has to leave you feeling unmoored."

Simone looked up with a wry smile. "It really does. After I sold the house, it was like… what is home anymore? I guess it's just Matilda and Skipper." She must have seen his confused expression. "Dad named the motorhome Matilda," she added.

"Ah. Thanks," he said. "I wasn't going to get that. I think home is really about the people and not the place. I think if my folks and Michelle moved, I'd probably feel lost."

"Yeah," said Simone, nodding. "That's how I feel. Lost. I mean, not all the time. I'm fine," she said, blushing. He got the feeling that Simone had invested a lot of time in convincing people she was okay.

"I think that's allowed," he said. "I think you can be fine and lost at the same time. That's a little bit like wine making. You put in effort and then rack the wine and hope you did the right things, but you won't know until years later. Isn't that life? Hoping you got it right and not really knowing until you get to the end?"

Simone laughed. "I like that. My life is a wine. Can I be champagne?"

"Full of bubbles and both sweet and tart? Sounds perfect," he said grinning. "Why don't you head into the other room? I've got some of the Barolo in there. Give me a second to wash up, and I'll walk you through it."

"OK," said Simone, turning around. Jordan hurriedly began to wash up. He scrubbed at his hands in the sink and then fumbled to get a breath mint and check his hair in the tiny cracked mirror over the sink.

"Is this it on the counter?" called Simone from the other room.

"Yeah," he called back. "Go ahead and pour some out for us. I'll be right there." He was pretty sure there was a wine key there somewhere. "It might need to breathe a minute anyway."

He realized his left elbow still had grease on it and he went back to the sink.

"Oh my God, it smells divine!" exclaimed Simone, and he grinned at himself in the mirror. If she liked the smell, she was going to love the taste.

He rounded the corner and realized that she hadn't poured out the Barolo. Instead, she'd poured a second glass from the cask on his work bench. She was smelling the glass the same way she'd taken in the scent of the grapes on her first day at the winery—with a soft, lovely expression that seemed to be savoring the entire moment.

"Oh," said Jordan, and she looked up at him with a questioning expression. "That's not the Barolo."

"Then what is it?" she asked, lifting the glass to the light and looking at the bright yellow color as it clung to the sides.

"Um, that's my experiment. A few years after I started working here, I brought in a farm who had never done grapes before. None of the other wineries would take a chance on them, but they've become one of our top producers. They've got this fantastic basalt-laced soil that gives a natural acidity and a beautiful minerality in the fruit. That first year, they gave me a great deal on several varieties we use for many of our wines, and they threw in some Chardonnay grapes. We weren't doing a Chardonnay that year, so I co-opted all of them for my experiment. I used a *sur lie* process on it."

"What's a *sur lie* process?" asked Simone.

"The wine is kept with dead yeast cells and then rotated periodically to mix it. If you do it too much, it tastes bad. Too little, and it's flat and pointless. So, for eight years, I've been crossing my fingers and hoping I got the timing right. This is the first year I brought it out to taste. I was thinking about putting it out to our wine club, but Mateo does *not* approve," he said wryly.

"I don't understand," said Simone, frowning. "Why wouldn't he approve?"

"It's a French process. We are an Italian winery. We do Italian wines. The wine may be wonderful, but I'm a heretic for even thinking French thoughts."

Simone giggled. "Don't tell him, but I think French thoughts all the time. Give me a rainy Saturday and my middle name is practically *ennui*."

Jordan laughed. "I don't think he cares that much really. I think he gets sort of hemmed in by his family history. But I'm an all-American mutt, so naturally, I'm a rebel."

"Naturally," said Simone, her eyes twinkling. "Eight years," she said, scrutinizing the glass of wine in her hand. "That's a long time."

"That's about how long I've been working toward the Decanter Classic Cup, too," said Jordan. "We've won some other things. Our wine is always well-reviewed, but this kind of win will put us on the international map. The last time we had an international win was when Mateo first took over. I've turned down other job offers to work here because I believe in Amante and I believe in Luckless. I know we can be the best and I want everyone else to know it too. I want to win this so bad I can taste it. And I really think I can do it with the Barolo."

He stopped talking, feeling like he'd just revealed too much.

"Everyone here cares so much," said Simone with a wide smile. "I love Luckless. You're going to win. I know it."

"You haven't even tasted the wine yet," protested Jordan.

"And when I taste it, I will still think you can win. I have loved every Amante wine I've tried. Not that I'm any judge of wine. But…" She paused and looked at the glass of wine in her hand. "Well, does that mean I don't get to try this one?"

She looked so disappointed that Jordan almost laughed.

"You know what? Sure. Go ahead. Try it. Tell me what you think."

He waited while she lifted the glass and took a small sip. She let it sit in her mouth for a long moment, tipped her head back, and swallowed. Then she took another, larger sip with a sigh of happiness.

"I take it you like it?" asked Jordan with a chuckle.

"Mmm-hmmm!" She took another sip and gave him a contented smile.

"What does it taste like to you?" asked Jordan, trying not to grin. Her reaction was his favorite kind—instant bliss.

"Oh, please don't ask me! I don't know any of the proper words. I kept blurting out things like *tastes like a pencil around the edges* at George."

"That's graphite," said Jordan, feeling surprised. George had said Simone had a good palate, but he hadn't given it much thought. "It comes from the soil that the grapes are grown in. If you can taste it, you're way ahead of a lot of people. We can give you the words. We can't give you the taste buds. Taste it again. Tell me what comes to mind. Give me anything. Taste is tied to smell and memory. I'm always interested in what people associate with wine flavors."

Simone appeared to think for a brief moment as she savored another sip. "It reminds me of my grandfather." She paused again and then smiled nostalgically as she took another sip. "When he came back from his last trip to France, he brought back a case of different wines. One Saturday, we all sat around, drank wine, and ate cheese in the garden for the entire day. I was seventeen, and I felt so sophisticated. I got to hear all the stories I wasn't supposed to hear, drink wine, and just… hang out. It was one of the best days of my life. That's what it reminds me of—that day in the garden. Flowers and hot sunshine and family. It's wonderful."

Jordan beamed. "Yeah," he said. "It's pretty good."

She looked surprised. "This is better than pretty good. It's amazing!"

Jordan felt a bit like he'd won the Classic Cup already. "I'll put some in a bottle for you. But I suppose we really ought to taste what we're here to taste." Jordan went to the counter, moved the label print samples, and grabbed the wine key and a bottle of the Barolo."

"What are those?" asked Simone, picking up the labels.

"Late is what they are," said Jordan. "We're supposed to pick the labels for the Barolo, but Mateo is dragging his feet. Those are the two options. I'm pushing for the new look, and he's still thinking about going with the classic Amante blue."

"Oh," said Simone. "That's a tough choice, but… I really like the new look. And if you win the Classic, it's got the perfect spot for a sticker to say that."

"Yes!" exclaimed Jordan, happy to finally have someone on his side. "Now, just be sure to tell Mateo that when you see him."

"I don't think my vote counts for much," said Simone with a laugh.

"I don't know," said Jordan. "It might count for more than mine. I'm just the guy they've known all their lives. You're someone new and shiny with new and shiny information."

"Do they really discount your opinion?" asked Simone, looking concerned. "That's not fair. You're the one doing all the work. You know this place backward and forwards."

Jordan felt a blush creep up his cheeks.

"It's not all the time," he said. "But sometimes they act like I'm still twenty-two and fresh out of college."

"That's why you were mad about Mateo hiring me, wasn't it?" asked Simone, and Jordan nodded.

"Yeah. Mateo made me manager, and I swear he hasn't taken my advice about anything since. When I heard he hired someone, I got hacked off and said the wrong thing."

"Completely understandable!"

"Might have been understandable, but I still wish I hadn't done it."

"It's all right," she said, smiling. "And I will tell Mateo I like the other label better."

"You should come with us to the print shop," said Jordan, suddenly struck by the idea. "I bet you could get some fun shots of the label being printed."

"Ooh!" Her eyes lit up, and she clapped her hands. "I'm so in!"

"Great!" said Jordan, popping the cork out of the wine bottle. "Let's toast to that."

Simone giggled. "I'm not sure that's really toast-worthy."

"When you're drinking the right wine," said Jordan, pouring wine into glasses, "with the right person, then anything is toast-worthy."

Simone

Simone snapped a few more pictures of the printing press while Jordan dialed his phone for the tenth time. She could tell he was really mad. She couldn't believe Mateo had stood them up for the label selection.

Simone had spent the morning with Caleb and the dogs and most of the afternoon in her office, determinedly working on marketing for the winery and stubbornly away from Jordan. She was a professional, and she would do a professional job.

But one twenty-minute drive to the print shop with Jordan, she suddenly was as giggly and stupid as a twelve-year-old. She was going to have to admit it—she had a crush on Jordan Ryan. And she kind of thought maybe he liked her too.

She glanced over her shoulder at Jordan. Although, at the moment, Jordan didn't look like he liked anyone.

"Is it really bad if the label doesn't get picked today?" Simone whispered to the press operator. He was a fiftyish guy in blue work overalls covered in different colored ink splotches. Simone wasn't entirely sure if the overalls had come with the name patch that read STAN or if that really was his name, but she thought that, all things considered, he looked like a *Stan*.

"If it doesn't get picked today, the ink won't be dry in time to put the labels on the bottles," said Stan. "I can work all night, but I can't change the drying time of ink. As it is, we won't be able to get all the bottles labeled before the Classic. We're only going to be able to get enough done for the Classic itself. Mateo's always been a late picker, but this is crazy even for him."

Jordan apparently got Mateo's voicemail again because he growled and slammed his phone down on the light table. Simone went back over to him.

"What do you want to do?" she asked. "Stan says we have to pick today."

"Yeah, I know," Jordan said. "We're actually holding up the process right now. They burned plates for both designs so they could start printing as soon as we picked."

He took a deep breath and let it out slowly.

"Is he going to be mad if you pick without him?" asked Simone. She didn't want friction between her new friends, but it sounded like the labels *had* to get picked.

"No," said Jordan. "He's going to be mad because I picked the new design instead of going with the classic look."

Simone grinned. "You're going to risk it?"

"It seems reasonable. Only people who show up get to vote," said Jordan. He turned to the pressman. "Let's run the new design."

"Coming up," said Stan with a nod.

A half-hour later, they were scrutinizing the first proofs.

"The color will intensify once we run the spot gloss," said the pressman. "But what do you think?"

Jordan squinted at the sheet of labels through the printer's loop.

"Want to look?" asked Jordan, looking up at Simone.

"Yes! I have no idea what I'm looking for, but yes." She bent over and squinted into the magnifying glass.

"You're looking to see if the separate colors are aligning with each other," he said. "That's called the registration. If the registration is off, you'll see one or more of the colors as a separate line."

"I don't see that," said Simone, squinting.

"That's because it's perfect. Run it just like that," he said to the pressman.

"You got it," Stan agreed. "Sign off in the corner of that sheet, if you please."

Jordan signed the proof, and the pressman made some notes and stuck it to the side of the press with a magnet. "I'll call you when we've got a batch for you."

"Thanks," said Jordan, then he turned to Simone. "Well, I guess that's that."

"I guess so," said Simone. "You should drive me to a restaurant," she said, feeling very bold. "So I can buy you a drink."

A smile flashed over his face. "Sounds great."

Jordan's non-convertible ride was a sensible gray Ford F150 and she liked the way he helped her up into it like she was delicate.

"Where do you want to eat?" asked Jordan, settling behind the wheel.

"Well, you probably know best since it's your town, but I have to admit that due to all the Italian-ness oozing out of the winery, I've been kind of craving Italian."

"Sorry," said Jordan. "I wish. But Papa Italia's went out of business a couple of years ago when the owner retired. Everyone in town is still sad about it."

"Nooooo!" wailed Simone mockingly, which made Jordan laugh. "OK," she said, instantly recovering. "What about that place with the palm trees? That looks fun."

"Don's Tiki Revenge," said Jordan with a nod. "They have drinks that come in child's plastic beach buckets."

"And that's a good thing?" Simone tried to weigh the pros and cons of beach bucket drinks.

"Depends on which stage of a break-up you're in," said Jordan wisely, and Simone laughed. "They also have great kalua pork sandwiches. We can go there."

An hour later, Simone was halfway through a bucket drink and halfway through an improvised bossa nova with Jordan dancing to a live band.

"You guys are doing great!" bellowed a man in a silk suit jacket and a fez. Somehow, his insistence that they join the local group of dancers on the dance floor had seemed reasonable. Simone suspected the beach bucket had made them easy targets.

"You should join the Lounge Lizards Dance Club!" His dance partner nodded eagerly before bopping toward the wide-mouthed tiki fountain.

"No," said Jordan, shaking his head. "Definitely not doing that."

Simone giggled. "I can't believe we're making this work."

"My parents did square dancing," he said. "That meant my sister and I had to be the extra partner set for their practices. You'd be amazed how far a box step and sense of rhythm will get you. Although, we are not mentioning the square dancing to anyone I ever went to high school with." Simone laughed and accidentally stepped too close, bumping into Jordan.

"I think I maybe shouldn't have had the bucket," she said.

"Buckets are the best," he replied.

"My aunt!" gasped Simone.

"What?" Jordan rightfully looked confused.

"I forgot I told her I'd eat dinner with her!"

"Oh." Jordan looked disappointed. "We've only ordered appetizers so far. I can take you home."

"Or... I could text her that I'm working late?" suggested Simone, feeling a twinge of guilt. "She's been catching up with a lot of old friends since she got here. It's probably fine."

"I will tell you all about the Classic and what to expect," said Jordan. "That probably counts as working for the five minutes I'm talking."

"Totally crucial information that I have to hear," said Simone.

"Totally," agreed Jordan and gave her a spin.

Back at the table, Simone used the twisty straw to drink from her yellow pail as she finished her pulled pork sandwich.

"So what should I expect from the Classic?" she asked.

"Lots of people. Lots of wine. Lots of people drinking and spilling wine."

"I had a tasting with George," said Simone.

"Yes, you said. Did you learn something?"

"Yes, I learned that my grandfather knew a lot about wine."

Jordan laughed.

"No, seriously! It's just that he ranted about a long list of things, and wine was one of his favorite topics, so I tuned him out a lot. Because you can only listen to so much about grapes."

"Oh," said Jordan, looking guilty.

"He would go on forever about acids and minerals."

"I mean..."

"He taught Agriculture Sciences. He also talked about the potato more than any one should."

"Who cares about potatoes?" said Jordan confidently.

"Not me," said Simone. "And Dad used to threaten to throw potatoes at him if he didn't change the subject."

Jordan laughed.

"But I..." Simone paused. "I was going somewhere with this. I think I'm a little drunk because I've forgotten."

"Your tasting with George and your grandfather's rants on dirt minerals, which I must admit, I would listen to."

Simone laughed.

"Yes, right. That's what I was saying. But I guess I thought that wine was complicated. I mean, making wine is complicated, but tasting wine does not seem that hard."

Jordan leaned across the table. "It isn't. People just try to make wine sound fancy so they feel cool. The absolute best part about wine is that there are so many types that there is a wine for every palate. Historically, it wasn't fancy. It was just what people drank. Now, it sometimes sounds like you need a degree to enjoy it. I hate that. I think it should be more accessible. I love that Mateo is devoted to having quality wines at multiple price points."

"Dang it," said Simone, rummaging through her purse. "I need to write that down. We're the winery for the common man!"

"No. Put the pen down," Jordan said, taking the pen away from her and shoving it back in her purse. "We're supposed to be fake working. Not real working. I want to know about you! I want to know about all the states you've been to and how you learned to be such a great photographer."

"Oh, the photography was from Mom. She loves film. After she and Dad got divorced, it was the way we connected. She still is one of the first to heart all my photos."

"Why didn't you go stay with her after your Dad died?" asked Jordan. "I probably shouldn't have asked that. It's none of my business."

"She's in Delaware. I have two younger half-siblings who are still in high-school. She offered. I said no. We're not close, and I think I'd rather stand on my own two feet."

"I admire that about you," said Jordan, and Simone blushed. "I love my family. I love being close to them, but standing on your own two feet in a town where everyone remembers when your feet were a size two is hard. And it takes a lot of courage to go out into the world and try something new."

"Sometimes it's really lonely," admitted Simone.

"I can see that it would be," he said. "Want to go for a walk and get less buzzed before we drive home?"

"Yes," agreed Simone instantly. Spending more time with Jordan sounded like the best way to spend an evening. "Is there somewhere to walk?" Not that it mattered. She would walk through a junkyard with him.

"There's an ice cream shop down the street."

"You really know how to take a girl for a walk."

"Well, we may not be the fanciest town in the world, but Luckless knows what it takes to make people happy."

"Wine and ice cream?" asked Simone.

"That does seem to be the secret," he agreed. He finished signing the bill and stood up. "May I escort you, *Signorina?*" he asked with a hilariously formal bow.

"No, no, no," said Simone, shaking her head. "That was Grandpa's other rant. We're French. I'm a *mademoiselle.*"

"Ah," said Jordan, laughing. "My mistake."

"But if *Monsieur* is taking me to ice cream, then *Signor* can be Italian if he wants."

"Can I just be Jordan, and you be Simone?" he asked, tucking her arm into his.

"Yes," said Simone, smiling up at him. "Yes, please."

Juliette hefted the paper grocery bag onto her hip and stared up at the dark wooden doors of the Amante family home. Shopping with Mateo had been a combination of easy familiarity and delightful discovery as they found out new things about the other. But faced with the looming and formal Amante house, Juliette found the past had crept far too much into the present. Mateo was chatting about something as he unlocked the door, but Juliette had lost the thread of the conversation. As the doors swung open, he finally realized she wasn't with him and turned back to look at her.

"What?" he asked puzzled.

"I was never allowed inside the house," said Juliette. "We always met out at the barn."

"Your father punched mine in the face! I couldn't bring you home!"

Juliette couldn't help laughing at the memory. The two men had clashed multiple times, but the argument that had driven the wedge between their families happened during the Founders Day celebration in front of half the town. At the time, it had been

the source of endless gossip and drama. Now, it just seemed ridiculous. The over-wrought passions of two grown men arguing
about wine after drinking too much of it.

"Well, then he shouldn't have said my father didn't know how
to grow grapes," said Juliette, poking the hornet's nest.

Matteo groaned and flailed his arms, the keys in his hand
jingling. "Honestly, I don't know how they ever worked together
in the first place. Dad always had to be right about everything."

"So did mine," said Juliette, nodding as she remembered a
few of her louder arguments.

Matteo stopped and looked around as if suspecting eaves-
droppers.

"Here," he grabbed the groceries and put them on the floor
inside the open door. Then he took her hand and pulled Juliette
toward the garden.

"What are we doing?" laughed Juliette.

"I've got something to show you."

He pulled her to the back of the house, where strings of
lights illuminated a lush garden with a warm golden glow and
velvet dark shadows.

"Oh," said Juliette. "This is lovely."

"This way," he said, leading her to the far corner, where a
twisting grape vine formed an archway over a gate. "This," he
said, plucking a grape from the left side, "is an Aglianico from the
Amante Estate. My *nonna* carried it over in a pot from Italy and
smuggled it through customs."

He handed the dusky purple-black fruit to Juliette, and she
put it in her mouth. The grape burst with a sweet flavor but had
a tang on her tongue.

"We used to make Sangiovese from it before we outgrew production rates and had to outsource our grapes. We still have a few
in the fields, though."

"It's beautiful," said Juliette.

"And this," he said, taking a grape from the right side, "is the unnamed Primitivo varietal that your father created and wanted to grow here."

He handed it to her, and Juliette stared at the grape in shock. She felt like she was holding her father's heart in her hand. He had been so zealous about wine and agriculture. He had always wanted to leave a legacy, and now here it was. It was such a small thing to mean so much.

"It grows well in California," said Juliette primly. "It could have done well here."

"It does do well here," he said. "I get a few bottles out of it every year."

"He said he'd gotten rid of all of the seedlings because, technically, they all belonged to Amante," said Juliette. "We assumed your father burned the rest."

"He chucked them in the compost pile," said Mateo. "But putting seedlings into compost to get rid of them is rather counterproductive. Honestly, I think he had a hard time destroying any grape plant and couldn't bring himself to really do it. I dug one back out after it sprouted. After a few years of hiding it in the barn, I came up here and put it in. He knew grapes better than anyone. He had to know what this was, but he never said a damn word."

"My father never worked at another winery. He went back to teaching," said Juliette. "He was so mad when I left the state for college, but considering we couldn't go ten seconds without arguing, I didn't think being on the same college campus would be beneficial. A bunch of college loans were infinitely worth the peace of mind."

"Sometimes I wish I had done the same," Mateo admitted with a shake of his head.

She turned the grape over in her hand. "I can't believe you kept it alive all these years."

"I'm stubborn," said Mateo. "Not as stubborn as *some* people, but..."

"I should throw this at you," said Juliette.

"I've got more ammo," he said, pulling a grape off the Amante side.

Juliette laughed and popped the grape into her mouth.

"What I'm attempting to say, in the most long-winded way possible," he paused to collect a few more grapes from both sides of the gate, "is it that you have roots here too, and you are welcome in my house."

"Well, OK," said Juliette. "Then show me the house."

"I'll start with the kitchen," he said, grinning.

"You did promise me dinner," she said, smiling back. "Although, I can't believe you've taken all afternoon off for me."

Mateo shrugged. "Jordan can handle anything that comes up except for possibly Simone. She is a Laurent tornado of productivity. I'm not sure if Jordan knows if he's coming or going around her. I don't understand how they got off on such bad footing. I was really hoping they would hit it off."

"Are you trying to set my niece up with one of your employees?" she demanded, unsure if she should be amused or not. She supposed it depended on how Simone felt about this Jordan person. Mateo spoke highly of him, but Simone seemed to have a good head on her shoulders. If she didn't like him, there had to be a reason.

"Not set up," protested Mateo. "More, gently nudge in his direction. He works too much. If you and I learned anything from our parents, it's that wine should *not* be everything in someone's life."

"Well, that's true," admitted Juliette.

"And Simone would be such a wonderful permanent addition to the winery."

"You are scheming to keep Simone in Luckless!"

"No, I'm scheming to keep *you* in Luckless," said Mateo with a grin. "Now, come watch me make you linguine."

Caleb

Caleb looked up from his novel as Juliette came dashing into the house through the back door and up the stairs. Moments later she was back down in sweats and threw herself onto the couch. She grabbed a novel off the end table and cracked it open to the middle. A split second later, Simone walked in the front door, humming a soft tune and carrying a bright yellow child's plastic beach bucket.

"Hello dear," said Juliette, looking up from the book. "Did you get everything done at work?"

"Oh," said Simone, freezing. "Yup. Got everything taken care of. How was your evening?"

"Oh, you know," said Juliette, waving the book in what Caleb thought was a masterful piece of non-lying lying.

"Sorry!" exclaimed Simone, looking guilty. "Did you get some dinner, at least?"

"I went to an Italian place with a friend. Don't give it another thought. You had work to do—it was important."

"Oh," said Simone, looking thoughtful. "Well, I'm glad you had a good time. Actually, I was kind of thinking about calling it an early night. All this getting up at a consistent time has been difficult on my semi-vacationing self."

Juliette laughed. "Of course! We can catch up tomorrow."

"Night then! Night, Caleb!"

"Good night," said Caleb.

Juliette waited until they heard the bedroom door close upstairs.

"If she was working late, I'll eat my hat," whispered Juliette. "I think a boy in a gray truck dropped her off."

"Judging by her beach pail, I'll bet she was out at Don's Tiki Revenge with Jordan Ryan, the enologist at the winery," said Caleb. "He's smart, talented, and extremely single, according to his sister."

"Ha!" exclaimed Juliette, looking pleased.

"Meanwhile," said Caleb, sitting up and dog-earring his page, "as I appear to be the only adult in this house, I should very much like to know where you were, young lady." He skewered Juliette with a stern eye. "I am the host, and I am not to be left out of the gossip."

Juliette chuckled and then bit her lip. "You promise you won't tell anyone? At least, not yet."

"Of course, innkeepers promise." He said, holding up his right hand.

"I was out with Mateo Amante," said Juliette.

"No!" gasped Caleb.

"We used to have a thing back when we were kids," said Juliette, looking slightly embarrassed. "But our fathers were in a feud, and we had to sneak around. When my parents said they were moving, I told Mateo that if he wanted me to stay, he'd better give me a reason. But he was in college and couldn't commit, so I left."

"Well, the lack of commitment trend seems to have lasted. He's been Luckless's most eligible bachelor for like four decades running. I would have said he was batting for my team and taken my shot, but his most recent girlfriend said he was just a stick in the mud who never wanted to leave Luckless."

Juliette shrugged. "Back then, getting married was everything. But I had the fancy party and big white dress. It was loads of fun, but the marriage was not. I don't need to do it again. And I realize now that what I really wanted was for him to stand up to his father. But he couldn't do it at the time. Anyway, I told Mateo I'd never come back, and I didn't."

"Until now!" Caleb was delighted with the soap opera unfolding under his very own roof. "And you've picked up right where you left off—struck by Cupid's arrow!"

"Well, not exactly right where we left off, but… I suppose it seems silly at our age."

"Nonsense!" exclaimed Caleb, affronted by the very notion. "Love at any age is a blessing. But why don't you want to tell Simone?"

Juliette sighed. "I screwed up. My brother and I had a falling out over my husband. They never got along. And when Charles got sick, we buried the hatchet. I thought things were all right between us, but every time I called, they both said they were fine and there was no reason to come out to Colorado. I should never have taken them at their word. By the time I realized they were never going to tell me to come, it was too late. I went to the funeral, but Simone was heads down, handling everything, and didn't want to talk. And we met up a few weeks ago in Oregon, but it wasn't enough. I want to connect with her, but she's so independent. Handles everything on her own! The Laurents take care of themselves! Laurent stubbornness, is what it is. Honestly, I don't know how you talked her into letting you help her."

"Oh, I didn't ask. I just told her I was doing it," said Caleb.

Juliette looked thoughtful. "I should do that with the motorhome. She seems so set on paying for it herself. But if she's enjoying working at the winery—"

"With Jordan," said Caleb, with a grin.

"Exactly," said Juliette. "So if she's enjoying it, then there's no reason she shouldn't come out of this with a little bit of a cushion. Anyway, I don't want her to think I didn't come here for her. It really was to help her."

"Mostly," said Caleb, chuckling.

"Mostly," agreed Juliette, looking embarrassed but still smiling.

CHAPTER 7
Gotcha Award

Jordan woke up and smiled. He'd gone to bed in the same state. Dinner, dancing, and ice cream with Simone had been the best evening he could remember in months. Possibly years.

He picked his way through the boxes in the dining room to the kitchen and made himself some eggs. He'd purchased the house after his promotion with the intention of making it someplace his family could gather. But moving and the crush had taken the wind out of his sails, and he still had boxes full of stuff and not enough furniture. He looked around and tried to picture how it would look to Simone. He didn't know, but he was certain her photos would look great in the living room.

Shoving his eggs into a tortilla, he ate on the way to the gym and breezed through a workout. On the way to the winery, he pulled into his favorite coffee shop and headed for the counter.

The coffee shop specialized in breakfast sandwiches that had never heard of the term low-calorie and coffee drinks that could keep someone awake even through the most boring lectures.

He had just placed his order when the bell above the door jingled. He glanced over his shoulder and instantly winced.

"Jordan Neil Ryan," said his mother, Cynthia Ryan. Today, his mother wore her tennis outfit, including the classic seventies terry cloth head and wristbands.

"Hey, Mom," he said as she came for her hug. "What did I do now?" he asked. He'd always done something.

"I was at my water aerobics class this morning with Jennifer

Arroyo, you know Stella's mom."

"Stella?" repeated Jordan.

"You were in pre-school together."

"Oh," said Jordan.

"Stella's sister Vita is friends with Lizzie Alcarez."

"That's nice?" Jordan didn't know what else to say.

"And last night, Lizzie was having drinks with Katie Finken-stein. You went to high school with her."

"Right. We went to Junior Prom," corrected Jordan, relieved to have someone in the story he actually recognized.

"Jordan," said the barista, breezing by, "your mocha will be up in a sec."

He nodded his thanks and tried to walk toward the pick-up counter, but his mother blocked his way.

"Yes, exactly. So you can imagine Katie's shock when she saw you sharing a beach bucket at Don's Tiki Revenge with a girl she didn't recognize!"

Jordan wanted to protest that they hadn't been sharing. He'd helped Simone finish her drink so she could take the bucket home. That was sharing in the same straw sense. Just friends helping each other out. But he wasn't sure that a rambling solilo-quy on the nature of sharing and beach buckets was going to get him very far with his mother.

"Well, we're a small town, but even you don't know every-one," said Jordan, sidling around the snack display. His caffeine was so close.

"Jordan! Are you really doing this to me?" Cynthia flailed and nearly knocked over a cup display.

"Doing what?" asked Jordan. He stabilized the cups and shuffled sideways along the counter like a crab, as he saw his iced mocha slide onto the bar. It was a vision of whip cream, choco-late, and cold, icy goodness. His mother moved between him and the promised land of caffeine.

"Who was the girl?" demanded his mother.

Jordan had no reason *not* to tell his mother about Simone. Except there was nothing to tell, and his mother would make a huge thing out of it. All of his life, she had made a massive fuss over whoever he was dating. Michelle had combatted the drama by never bringing anyone home. He was convinced that Michelle would have eloped if she could have. Of course, Graham adored Cynthia and all the fuss she made, much to Michelle's chagrin.

"She's just the new employee at the winery," he said, stretching out his arm, trying to angle around his mother.

"New employee?" repeated Cynthia.

His fingertips slipped off the condensation on the plastic cup.

"Marketing coordinator. She's making the winery look more professional. She's already improved our social media. I think we've gone up over a hundred followers in the last two days."

"The Facebook did suggest that I like them yesterday."

"Mom!"

"What?" She looked genuinely confused as to what had upset him.

"You didn't already like us?"

"Well, I mean, you're a bit boring. I didn't want that stodginess cluttering up my feed. You don't have any cute animals at all."

"Mom!"

"I admit that it did look more interesting this time around. The photos were lovely. Is that because of this new girl?"

"Yes," said Jordan, feeling annoyed. "She's a brilliant photographer."

"And extremely pretty, according to Katie Finkelstein."

Jordan's hand finally wrapped around the side of his iced mocha.

"I have to go to work, Mom." He slid around his mother and headed for the door.

"But you haven't told me anything about her," protested Cynthia.

"Co-worker," said Jordan.

"You don't share buckets with co-workers," said Cynthia, narrowing her eyes.

"Gotta go, Mom!" Jordan hurried out the door, rushing to avoid more awkward questions.

"I'm calling your sister!"

"Good luck!" Jordan called back. Michelle was his ally and could give a CIA operative a run for their money in a keeping her mouth shut competition.

He arrived at the winery at the same time as Laureen, who had volunteered to drive Simone to work since Sir Barkington's was on her way.

"Hi!" said Simone, getting out of the car.

"Jordan, honey," said Laureen, climbing out of the driver's seat. "I had a thought on the way over. I love all of Simone's pictures, but what if we put the spotlight on our field crews? Couldn't you take her around and introduce her to some of the teams?"

"Yeah, absolutely," said Jordan and watched Laureen smirk at his enthusiasm. "I'd love to highlight Santiago. He never wants recognition, but without him, we couldn't function."

"Oh, fantastic," said Simone, grabbing Skipper's leash as he hopped out of the car. "I'm trying to put together a series on winery employees. I'd like to make it so we're not constantly scrambling for content. It would be great to schedule at least a few weeks in advance."

"You can do that?"

The slightly stunned look on Simone's face said that was a

stupid question. Even Skipper looked up from peeing on a rogue dandelion in the gravel lot.

"You've been posting everything live prior to me working here?"

Jordan shrugged. "I don't know. I guess I thought so? That's not how it's done?"

"No," said Simone, and he could tell she was trying not to laugh.

"Oh, well. Then it's good that you're here."

Laureen chuckled. "Understatement. Simone, I'll see you later. Jordan, don't keep her all day. We do actually have a few things to do in the office."

Laureen headed to the office and Jordan looked to see what Simone thought of the plan.

"I guess you're going to take me for another walk?" she asked, stepping closer.

"You don't mind, do you?" he asked, grinning. "I know where George hides the ice cream sandwiches so I can make it worthwhile."

"I don't know… Walking is great, but dancing was pretty good too."

"Shh! We're keeping that under our hats. I don't dance, and I never wore a bolo tie."

"And Michelle never wore a fluffy petticoat?" asked Simone, laughing.

"Exactly!"

"But I liked dancing," protested Simone. Jordan had to pause and reconsider his stance on dancing. A pretty girl had just told him she wanted to dance with him. Why wasn't he making plans right this second?

"Then we should do it again, but it's a hard no on the tie, and I'm not joining the lounge lizards club or whatever they were."

"No clubs," she said, grinning. "Just you and me."

"Done," he agreed, then gathered his courage. "Maybe after the Classic? Unless you're doing something with your aunt." He added the last part hastily to give her an easy out.

"We can celebrate our win," she said confidently and he couldn't help noticing that she was blushing.

"Knock on wood," he said fervently.

"Although," she stopped with a frown. "I think something funny is going on with Aunt Juliette. She lied to me!"

"About what?"

"I'm not sure, but she said she went out to dinner with friends."

"OK?"

"Yes, but she said they went to an Italian restaurant!"

"But there isn't one anymore," said Jordan, puzzled.

"I know!" she exclaimed, and Skipper let out a sharp bark as if to underline the point.

Simone

Simone finished her last website update and closed out her browser. Sensing that leaving was imminent, Skipper stretched in his bed and shook himself.

"Ooh, big stretch," said Simone, as the Good Dog Owner's Handbook required. "Ready to go home? Or at least back to Sir Barkington's?"

It was surprising how fast the bed and breakfast had come to feel like a secure home base. Her morning with Jordan out in the fields had been a delight. She now had stacks of photos and content that she could use after the Classic. She wasn't sure what her employment status would be then, but she wanted to leave them with at least a month's worth of pre-scheduled posts. It seemed like the least she could do after everyone had been so kind. Particularly, Jordan.

Simone sighed. Jordan had been so wonderful. She got the feeling that he was trying to make her fall in love with wine. He was going out of his way to show her everything that went into making wine. But all that was accomplishing was making her fall in love with Jordan. His passion made him more attractive than anyone she'd met in the last year.

But that just left Simone in confusion. She was on her way back to Colorado. There was a plan. Not a very good one or one that she particularly liked, but it was a plan. Was she supposed to throw caution to the wind because a boy looked at her a particular way or because he tried to show her his favorite grapes?

For a moment, she contemplated talking to her aunt about the situation. But what if Juliette just laughed it off as a crush? She was so sophisticated and probably wouldn't take Simone's feelings seriously. They were family, but they weren't really that close, were they?

Simone reached the front lobby and saw an older woman in a tennis dress surveying the empty front desk. Her hair was clipped in a stylish frosted bob, and she had an athletic, energetic aura.

"Hello," said Simone. "Can I help you?"

"Hi," said the woman, holding out her hand. "I'm Cynthia."

"Simone." They shook hands, and Simone felt like she was being inspected from her toes to the top of her head.

"I wanted to drop something off for Jordan, but Laureen's not in."

"She goes home early on Thursdays," said Simone. "But I can take it."

"You must be new," said Cynthia.

"Yes, I'm the new marketing coordinator," said Simone.

"Ah, you're responsible for all the new stuff on their social media. That's great. How do you like working at the winery?"

"Oh, it's been wonderful," said Simone. "Everyone has been so nice to me."

"Just moved to Luckless?"

"Oh, no. I'm here for a visit. Or at least I was. But my motorhome broke down, and I needed a job so I could pay for the repairs. I'm helping get the winery through the Classic."

"Well, of course, but I mean…" Cynthia leaned forward conspiratorially. "They obviously need long-term help. Have you thought about staying?"

"I…" Simone felt pinned in place by Cynthia's inquiring hazel gaze. "Well, honestly, I have been thinking about it a bit. Jordan keeps taking me to fun places and it would be nice to have someplace to belong to again." She blushed, realizing that she had said more than she intended.

"Luckless is a nice town," said Cynthia, smiling confidently. "And Jordan is a smart boy. Anyway, if you could give this to him, I would appreciate it."

Cynthia handed over a paper grocery bag.

"What is it?" asked Simone, peering inside. It looked like a cheap bowling trophy.

"Oh, it's the Gotcha Award. Don't worry, he'll know what it's for. We pass it around pretty often."

"Well, OK," said Simone, still feeling puzzled.

Juliette

Juliette exited her rental car and looked up at the Amante Winery nervously. A woman in a tennis dress was walking down the path.

"They're still open," she called as she approached. "Go up to the tasting room. You'll get the best wine in the state—promise!"

"Thanks," said Juliette. "I'm meeting someone."

"Couldn't pick a better spot," said the woman with a breezy smile as she headed for her car. Juliette watched her leave, envying her carefree attitude.

There was a path from the lot up to the tasting room and it forked off to another building that was probably the office. Mateo had told her to meet him in the winery.

It wasn't that she didn't want to tell Simone about Mateo. It was that she didn't want to tell anyone. She felt silly to dive so fast into something that had already broken her heart once. She didn't want to justify herself or admit that she had no intention of listening to reason. Mateo felt different from their youth and yet also so familiar and right.

She was almost to the tasting room door when Simone called her name.

"Juliette!"

Hand outstretched for the door handle, Juliette froze.

"Simone!" she said, turning around and plastering a smile on her face.

"Hey, Simone!"

A young man hurried from the direction of the far buildings and waved at Simone. Simone waved back with the hand holding Skipper's leash. She was carrying a grocery sack in the other.

"What are you doing here?" asked Simone, turning back to Juliette. Skipper bounded ahead of her niece, and Juliette bent down to give him his requisite pets and herself time to think.

"Glad I caught you!" said the young man, smiling as he approached.

"I was passing by and thought I'd see if you wanted a ride home," said Juliette.

"Oh." Simone glanced guiltily over her shoulder at the sandy-haired young man, and Juliette tried not to laugh. Simone was as transparent as glass.

"Juliette, this is Jordan Ryan," said Simone, gesturing between them. "The Amante Winery enologist."

"It's so nice to meet you," said Jordan, stepping forward to shake her hand.

"You're not Italian," said Juliette, scrutinizing his face. From the way Mateo spoke about him, it was clear that Jordan was who Mateo was intending to pass control of the winery to, and Juliette was surprised to see that he wasn't at all Italian looking. He had a square-jawed All-American kind of look.

"Uh, no?" Jordan looked confused.

"Sorry, when I was growing up, Mateo's father was convinced that only Italians knew how to make wine. I'm surprised the Amante enologist wouldn't be Italian."

"Ah," said Jordan, nodding. "Yes. Mr. Amante was still alive when I started working here. We had to tell him that my family was Northern Italian. Very, very northern. England was part of the Roman Empire at some point, right?"

Juliette laughed in surprise.

"His mind had started to go by then. Unless you were talking about wine. In which case, he was still sharp as a tack. I got his approval based on wine knowledge and three sentences of Italian."

"He was very set in his ways," said Juliette.

"Yes," agreed Jordan, "but fortunately, Mateo is not like that."

"That's good to hear," said Juliette.

"Oh," said Simone. "Jordan, someone dropped this off for you." She held up a paper grocery sack.

Jordan took the bag and pulled out a plastic gold and faux wood bowling trophy. He immediately groaned.

"She said her name was Cynthia, and you would know what it was for."

"Yes. That was my mother, and I know exactly what it's for," he said, shaking his head.

"Oh," said Simone, looking surprised. "She did say you were a smart boy."

Jordan gave an embarrassed laugh. "I'll call her later."

Behind the pair, Juliette saw Mateo coming out of the office building. He froze as he saw who she was talking to.

"Hey, um," Jordan glanced at Simone, "I was actually going to take Simone to check the first batch of labels at the bottler."

"Oh!" exclaimed Simone, her hands flapping urgently. "I want pictures of that!"

Juliette laughed at Simone's excitement. "Do you want me to take my grand-nephew back to Caleb's?"

"Your grand-nephew?" laughed Simone.

"Well, he is my cutest little angel baby," cooed Juliette, scrubbing at Skipper's ears. Skipper looked like this was the kind of treatment he expected.

"Well, yes," agreed Simone, "that's true. He *is* an angel baby." Jordan laughed which earned a stern look from Simone.

"Angel baby," he agreed, holding up his hands in instant surrender.

"I can take him home if you want to get pictures," said Juliette.

"Can you?" asked Simone guiltily.

"No problem," said Juliette. "I look forward to the photos. Your social posts have been great. Such an improvement."

"You followed Amante before?" asked Jordan, looking surprised.

"Oh, it's a hometown winery," said Juliette. "How could I not?"

"My mom didn't even follow us," he said drily.

"What? No!" Simone looked offended. "She said the posts were great."

"She probably looked before she came over, but this morning, she said we didn't have enough cute animals," said Jordan.

"Oh, shoot. We really don't. Maybe we can do an employee pets day."

"Well, I'll let you sort that out," said Juliette. "I'll just take this employee pet right here." She took the leash out of Simone's hand.

"Be good for Aunt Juliette, Skipper!" said Simone.

"Skipper knows I will feed him all the biscuits," said Juliette. "Although, is the shop still open? Maybe I'll just pop in and get a bottle to take home. And can I take Skipper with me?"

"Yeah, we're dog-friendly. Just head inside," said Jordan. "Oh, look, there's Mateo."

He waved, and Mateo tentatively waved back.

"Do you want me to introduce you, Aunt Juliette?" asked Simone.

"Oh, you two go ahead," said Juliette. "The bottler probably can't wait forever."

"Thanks, Aunt Juliette," said Simone, throwing her arms around Juliette in an impulsive hug. For a moment, Juliette was overwhelmed with a keen sense of belonging. She hugged Simone back tightly.

"Of course, sweetie."

Simone stepped back, beaming, and Juliette vowed that she would head to the garage the next day to pay off the motorhome bill. Simone deserved to have someone take care of her for a change.

She watched the pair get into Jordan's gray truck and then walked up the path to meet Mateo.

"Where are they off to?" asked Mateo, staring at Jordan's truck.

"He's taking Simone to get pictures of the bottling plant."

"We don't need to check on that," said Mateo with a frown. "We've worked with the same bottler for years. He knows what he's doing."

"Yes, but it's the perfect thing to take the new Marketing Coordinator to see," said Juliette. "You know, if you were looking for an afternoon event that might turn into dinner."

"Ohhhhh," said Mateo nodding. "Yes, of course. Obviously crucial for Simone to see that. I guess that means we've got the evening to ourselves."

"Not entirely," said Juliette, gesturing to Skipper. "We're babysitting my grand-nephew."

"That is fine," said Mateo, bending down to scratch the little dog's ears. "He can come on our picnic."

"Aren't we a little old for a picnic?" asked Juliette skeptically.

"You're thinking of heat, bugs, and dirt," said Mateo, nodding sagely.

"Well..." Juliette shrugged her agreement.

"I'm thinking of charcuterie and wine on a boat in a lake with a sunset."

"Ohhhhh," said Juliette. "That's not a picnic. That's a romantic evening without a care in the world."

"Now you're getting the picture," said Mateo, smiling broadly.

Simone

Simone took an extra few shots of the bottles and labels. The repetition of shapes and colors created a superb composition. She glanced up and realized that Jordan was playing on his phone and clearly waiting on her.

"Sorry," said Simone, blushing.

"For what? Making art?" he asked, looking up. "Don't apologize for that."

Simone stared at him. "I don't think anyone's called my photos art before."

"Uh… Are people blind?"

"No, but I've always been a photo nut and people get impatient with me wasting time to get the perfect shot."

"I learned pretty early on that people always want things faster. But I can't let someone else push my timeline on making wine. It takes what it takes. It's your job to make the winery look great, and your photos are art. Both of those things deserve respect. The next person who tries to rush you can come talk to me."

Simone couldn't help smiling.

"I might do that," she said. "I don't suppose you want to take me to dinner again? I'm starving."

"Absolutely. I was thinking of Antojos. It's close to Caleb's. I'll walk you home, and we can work off the cookies we'll get at the bakery that's on the way."

Simone laughed. "I truly love your style of walking."

"I really only walk to the next dessert," he said with a grin.

In true Luckless fashion, the bakery was peak cute with pink walls and a confection of lace curtains and trim, but the back wall was filled with sensible baguettes and sourdough rounds.

They walked toward Caleb's nibbling their cookies and Simone couldn't help feeling that Luckless had delivered up another perfect day. They rounded the corner and Simone could see Sir Barkington's at the end of the block. The light strands in the backyard were lit, and Simone could hear laughter echoing in the warm evening air. Caleb's house was a happy one, and it made Simone smile.

Their pace slowed as they approached the front porch, and Simone searched for something to say. Jordan's hand connected with hers, and Simone felt her heart rate pick up. She hoped her palms weren't sweating. They walked for a few moments in silence until they reached the front steps of Sir Barkington's.

"You know, if... um..." Jordan pulled her to a stop, and Simone stared up into his hazel eyes. "If we're really going dancing, I should probably..."

"Probably?" prompted Simone breathlessly. She didn't know what he was trying to say. She wasn't even sure what she was trying to say.

"I should know what kind of music you like," he said.

Simone wanted to laugh. His entire face said that hadn't been what he meant to say.

"All kinds," she said, going up on her tip-toes and leaning against his chest.

"Oh, OK," he said, nodding, but his arm slid around her waist. He was getting the hint.

The evening breeze snuck by with a little whisper of sweetness. Simone tilted her head, and Jordan leaned down to match her and pressed a kiss into her lips. The night seemed like velvet silence and Simone could swear she felt his heart beat against hers.

There was a burst of noise as the front door was flung open. Jordan and Simone jumped apart as Caleb came out onto the porch.

"Simone! You're home!"

"Yes," said Simone. "Just got here. Jordan walked me home."

"Because he's a gentleman," said Caleb confidently. "Come on in. I'm serving wine for the new guests. But I forgot Sir Barkington's biscuits out here on the porch."

"I can't stay," said Jordan, and Simone heard the laughter in his voice. "Simone, I'll see you tomorrow?"

"Yes," said Simone shyly.

"Good," he said. "Good night, Caleb."

"Night, Jordan!" Caleb was already heading inside with the biscuit plate.

"Good night, Jordan," said Simone softly as Jordan began to walk back toward his car.

"Good night, Simone," he said with a flashing smile that lit up Simone's heart.

CHAPTER 8
Heading for the Crash

Simone

Simone confidently stepped out of Sir Barkington's with six leashes in her hands and pockets full of dog treats and bags for any *deposits* made by the pups. The event had officially arrived, and everyone who traveled with their dog seemed to have brought their pooches to Caleb. She was now on morning and evening walk patrol.

Simone waved at one of Caleb's neighbors and felt smug when he waved back. Luckless was the friendliest little town. She walked down toward the park with a wide gravel walking path and shady trees, stopping periodically when the pack decided that a smell just could not be ignored.

She tried to walk on the very edge of the path to make way for morning joggers, but one ran up and stopped.

"Hey!" exclaimed Michelle Ryan, putting her hands on her hips and panting.

"Hey!" said Simone. "Look at you being all fit! I think all I've done lately is walk dogs and drink wine."

Michelle laughed. "Yeah, wait till you have kids. Then you'll take up jogging just to get twenty minutes to yourself. My kids are the best, but it's like they think I'm a PB and J dispenser combined with a TV. Although, they *are* my little snuggle dispensers so it probably comes out even."

"That is some real talk on motherhood," said Simone. "I feel like I should be taking notes."

Michelle grinned. "I tell it like it is, but don't let that scare you off. Kids are ridiculous amounts of fun. I laugh all the time. Sometimes when I'm not supposed to, but still."

That made Simone laugh. "I'll keep that in mind."

"I actually did have a reason for stopping," said Michelle. "I talked to your aunt this morning. We're all squared away on the bill, but I forgot to tell her that the last of the parts won't be in until tomorrow."

"Squared away…" repeated Simone.

"I can get it done tomorrow after they arrive, but you're not in a hurry, right? Jordan said you're staying here through the event."

"Yeah," said Simone. "I'm definitely staying through the event."

"It's great that you got a job at Amante," said Michelle cheerfully. "Jordan's been wanting someone for ages. He's really happy you're here."

"Is he?" asked Simone, unable to stop herself from smiling at that comment.

"Oh, yeah. He was saying you're a social media genius."

"I wouldn't go that far," said Simone.

"He would," said Michelle with a smirk. "Anyway, I'll give you a call when the repairs are done. I'll see you guys later. I think Graham and I are on tap for free labor shifting boxes or something when you guys set up for the event."

"Oh, that's great," said Simone. "Thanks!"

Michelle laughed. "Yeah, well, I'm pretty sure we owe him for the weeks-worth of childcare from earlier this summer. Jordan helps out with everything."

"He does, doesn't he?" said Simone. "I swear he's the winery's resident problem solver."

"Yeah, sometimes I think people get a little too used to relying on him instead of solving their own problems, but Jordan hates to tell people no. Not that I want him to tell me *no* on babysitting. Mama likes her date nights."

"He's really sweet," said Simone.

"He really is," agreed Michelle. "Anyway, I'd better finish my jog before the house goes up in fire due to a lack of mom. See ya!"

"Bye!" said Simone as Michelle jogged off.

She waited until Michelle was way out of earshot before pulling her phone from her pocket and dialing Juliette. But it went straight to voicemail.

"This is Juliette. Wait for the beep and leave a message, or just text me if you're feeling millennial!" The phone beeped and Simone struggled to not sound angry.

"Hey Juliette," said Simone. "Um… I just talked to Michelle. She said that you had taken care of the bill on Matilda. The motorhome, I mean. Um… I really wish you'd talked to me. I don't want… Um… Just call me back."

Jordan

Jordan fidgeted by the front door of the bat cave and waited for Simone. He knew she was getting a ride with Laureen this morning, but he didn't want to wait in the office. He knew he'd get raised eyebrows from Laureen for that, so he kept an eye on the parking lot and waited. He saw Laureen's car park, and both women got out. He stepped outside and waved toward the car, hoping Simone would get the hint.

He saw her turn and say something to Laureen, and then she began to jog across the lot toward the barn, Skipper bounding gleefully along at her side.

"Hey!" she exclaimed, slowing to a walk as she got closer.

"Hey," he said, smiling involuntarily. "Laureen is still staring at us."

"She's probably under instructions from Caleb," said Simone with a wry smile.

"I forgot to grab you a bottle of the *sur lie* chardonnay the other day," said Jordan loudly, and Simone's eyes began to dance in laughter. "Did you want one?"

"Ooh! Yes!" Her response could not have been more enthusiastic. "Caleb is going to lose his mind if I let him have some."

"Was that an *if?*" asked Jordan, laughing as he entered the barn.

"Definite if," said Simone.

"Hi," said Jordan when the door was shut.

"Hi," said Simone.

He wasn't sure if kissing was the correct greeting, but he knew he wanted it to be. Throwing caution to the wind, he leaned in for a kiss, and Simone instantly responded by wrapping her arms around his neck.

It might have been a minute or an entire later that he felt Skipper crash into his leg.

"Skipper!" Simone shook her finger at the little dog, who had found a tennis ball from somewhere. Jordan chucked the ball into the dusty car side of the barn.

"It's OK. We probably can't spend forever doing that. I actually do want to talk to you."

"Yeah?" Simone's eyebrows went up sharply and he realized he'd inadvertently used a break-up kind of phrase. "I wanted to ask about your aunt," he said quickly. "And you really do want some wine, right?"

"Absolutely on the wine," said Simone, relaxing. "And ugh!" Simone flapped her arms and looked strangely angry. "Oh, I'm so mad at her! She definitely lied to me about getting Italian for dinner the other night. And I tried to talk to Caleb about it, but he completely avoided me. She obviously got to him before me. I don't know what she thinks she's doing."

"Well," said Jordan, "she might have had Italian. But it wasn't from a restaurant."

"What?" Simone frowned.

"I stopped by the Price Mansion this morning to talk to Linda about something, and she said she saw Juliette and Mateo at the grocery store last night buying stuff for dinner."

"No!" gasped Simone, her anger dissipating in favor of shock.

"She also said that the two of them used to be an item back when your aunt lived here, but they broke up when she moved."

"Well!" said Simone, looking affronted. "She never said a word! And dinner in? That's… fast. That feels fast, doesn't it?"

"It's a little fast," admitted Jordan. "But I mean… What if they're in love?"

Simone looked up at him with big, worried eyes. "It could be love," she said. "But they live in different states. How is it going to work?"

"Couldn't she move, maybe? Does she really need to go back to Colorado?"

"She lives in Oregon," said Simone.

"Right," said Jordan. "Right. I meant Oregon."

"Maybe she could move," said Simone. She scuffed at the floor with the toe of her sneaker. "She doesn't have a job. I mean, she's retired, so maybe it wouldn't be that big of a deal."

"Luckless is a pretty good town," offered Jordan, hopefully. "She could be happy here. It's a good place to call home."

"I like Luckless," said Simone, smiling. Then she frowned. "Only…"

"Only, what?" asked Jordan, feeling a nervous lump in the pit of his stomach. He turned his back and rummaged around for a cork for the bottle.

"I also found out my aunt paid for the repairs on the motorhome. I didn't want her to do that! I just wanted a little bit because she promised she'd pay for some of Dad's funeral."

"Oh no! She paid for everything! The absolute horror," said Jordan, shoving a cork in the bottle top.

"I know it sounds silly, and I know Juliette was trying to be nice, but I wish she'd talked to me first. I don't like owing people."

"She's your aunt," said Jordan. It didn't seem like that big of a deal to him.

"Yeah," said Simone. "I don't know. Maybe I'm just being too stubborn. Laurents are known to do that occasionally."

"Oh," he said, smiling. "Is that what they're known for?"

"And our charm," she said, wrinkling her nose at him.

"Well, it doesn't mean you get to leave if that's what you're thinking," Jordan said, attempting to sound arrogant. "I'm the manager, and I happen to know that you're supposed to stay for at least the next week. You can't leave, or we'll sue you for breach of contract."

"I don't think I'm going anywhere," she said shyly. "It just means that when Michelle finishes the repairs, I'll have to find someplace to park the motorhome. I have no idea where to put it."

Jordan couldn't help thinking he had a great spot next to his house, but didn't say that.

"I'm sure Mateo will let you park it up here, if nothing else. You can pop it in next to the Spider."

"Really? I swear you fix everything," said Simone, which made him feel about ten feet tall.

"Hey, Jordan!" called someone from outside.

"In here," Jordan yelled back in the general direction of the open door.

"Hey," said George, leaning in. He scrutinized Simone for a sliver of a moment. "I just talked to the labeler. They're put the first batch of the Barolo on a truck. It'll be here late tonight. But at least that'll be in time. I was starting to sweat it there."

"You and me both," said Jordan. "Are we going to have enough people to unload?"

"Probably not," said George. "I can roust anyone who wants overtime, but I think we're kind of going to be short."

"I'll call Michelle," said Jordan. "I already warned her. She knows she and Graham owe for babysitting that entire week in June."

George chuckled. "You looked like you'd been run over by a truck."

"That's about how I felt. But with them and us, and if we get a couple of extra hands, we should be OK."

"I'm in," said Simone.

"Great," said George. "We'll get it done in no time. Decanter Cup, here we come!"

"We're so going to win," said Simone confidently.

"I hope we're that lucky," said Jordan.

"I think we definitely are," said Simone, taking a few steps back down the path. "I'll see you tonight."

Simone

Simone waited on the front porch of Sir Barkington's. The afternoon had been hot, and she was still sweaty from her walk with Marmaduke the Great Dane. But a bit of cloud cover had swept in, turning the evening chilly. Simone pulled her hoodie tighter around herself and snuggled Sir Barkington and Skipper closer to her on either side. Skipper didn't mind—two-a-day walks and free run of the winery had kept the little dog away from his usual four-a-day naps. Sir Barkington grumbled and smacked his lips but didn't go to the actual effort of waking up. Inside, Caleb was chatting with the tide of other guests who had come in for the event. Simone had chosen to get out of his way and come out to the porch to wait for Juliette.

"Don't you look snuggly," said Juliette, coming up the walk. "Are we still on for dinner? I thought you might have to work late tonight, too."

"I do, actually," said Simone. "The Barolo is coming in tonight and we need to go unload it, break it down, and load everything onto a truck for the event tomorrow. Jordan's going to pick me up in a bit, but I needed to talk to you."

Juliette sighed. "You're mad about the motorhome, aren't you?"

"You weren't supposed to pay for the whole thing!" exclaimed Simone.

"Why not? Seriously, sweetie. Why not? Wouldn't your Dad pay for it if he were here?"

"Dad would have fixed it himself," said Simone. "And I'm trying…" Her voice gave out, and a tear trickled down her face. Angrily, she wiped at the tear and tried to fight the flood of emotion back down.

Juliette came over and picked up Sir Barkington, moving him to another chair before sitting down and putting her arms around Simone.

"You don't have to be all grown up, sweetie. You're allowed to be someone's baby even when you're twenty-six."

"No, I'm supposed to handle things," protested Simone. "I took care of Dad. And I took care of the funeral and selling the house. I can take care of the stupid motorhome, too."

Juliette leaned back and looked at her. "What do you mean you took care of selling the house?" she demanded sharply.

"I had to," said Simone. "The medical bills and the funeral and then my student loans. This trip was the last of it. That's why I had to get a job."

"Simone!"

"I had to," protested Simone. "Dad said I should. He had money set aside, but he knew it wouldn't be enough. As it was, I still got a new bill from the hospital two months ago. Dad wanted to make sure I wasn't going to start life with a pile of debt."

Juliette threw her hands in the air in frustration. "Why didn't you call me? Why didn't either of you stubborn stupid Laurents call me?"

"And say what? Hey, Aunt Juliette, can I come live at your house? What, you never wanted to have a mid-twenties slacker living in your basement? Too bad!"

"Don't be ridiculous," said Juliette. "I don't have a basement. I'd have to put you in the tiny room under the eaves and slip you food through a slot in the door."

Simone stared at her aunt. "Well, now you're just being silly," she said primly.

"Yes, I am," said Juliette. "And so are you. Why wouldn't you come live with me? Or why wouldn't I help you with the finances? I know we weren't close when you were growing up, and that's my fault. I should have made more of an effort. But we're the only family we have left. I love you."

"Oh," said Simone, her bottom lip wobbling. "I love you too." She managed to get the words out, but barely and then lunged forward to hug her aunt.

"You will always have a home with me," said Juliette, hugging her tight. "I promise."

Simone barely managed to not break down entirely, but it was only by scrunching her eyes closed as tight as possible and leaning into her aunt's shoulder.

"Although," said her aunt, clearing her throat, "I have been wondering if maybe you were thinking about making your stay in Luckless a little longer. You've been having such a good time at this job. And Luckless is a very nice town."

"You're just saying that because you're dating Mateo," said Simone, through her aunt's hair.

"Caleb ratted me out!"

"No," said Simone, sitting up. "The Italian restaurant went out of business two years ago, and Linda Thornton saw you at the grocery shopping with him the other night."

"Small town gossip is the fastest thing on earth," said Juliette. "They ought to figure out how to harness it as a form of renewable energy."

Simone giggled, then turned serious. "Are you sure about this, Aunt Juliette?"

"Sweetie, I was sure forty years ago. He was the one who wasn't certain. *I was French, he was Italian. What would our parents say?*"

"Grandpa was kind of stuck on that," said Simone reflectively.

"Those things mattered back in those days. That's one of the things I'm happy we've moved on from. Anyway, Mateo wanted more time to *think*." Juliette rolled her eyes. "But we were moving and I wasn't going to delay starting my life for the hope that maybe someday Mateo Amante might get around to asking me to marry him."

"He should have put a ring on it," said Simone firmly.

"Thank you," said Juliette with a nod. "But water under the bridge. We're here now. And I think this time, we're both on the same page. So," she paused to clear her throat, "what I'm saying is that if you want to live with me, you may have to stay in Luckless whether you want to or not. Or I may be moving into Matilda with you."

"Skipper and I would be happy to have you," said Simone. "But, fair warning, he snores."

Juliette laughed. "Good to know. Is that your young man?" she asked, pointing out to the curb where Jordan had pulled up in his gray truck.

"That is Jordan," said Simone, eyeing her aunt suspiciously.

"Mm-hmm," said Juliette, her eyes twinkling. "Mateo speaks very highly of him."

"He's kind of the best," said Simone. "A little bit of a temper if he's working on a car, but other than that, kind of…"

"Dreamy?" suggested Juliette.

"I'm going to work now," said Simone, getting up. "Come on, Skipper."

"It's OK to take a risk, you know," said Juliette as Simone went down the stairs. "Don't wait for the perfect time. There's no such thing."

Simone looked back at her aunt. "Thanks, Aunt Juliette," she said with a smile.

"I'll see you when you get home," said Juliette with a wave. "Love you."

"Love you too," said Simone, and went down the walk to Jordan's truck feeling happier than she had in months.

PART 3:

It's Complicated...
Italian Wine
in French Barrels

We recommend pairing this section with a Sangiovese. It carries an intensity, yet dances with a lightness that echoes the soul of Tuscany. American Sangiovese, in its pursuit of perfection, embraces French oak barrels with the same passionate resolve as Jordan, crafting the perfect glass.

Our pick the 2015 Sangiovese from Leonetti Cellar.

TASTING NOTES: The nose is flamboyant with graham cracker, pureed raspberries, tar, and cigar box. Rustic, perfectly polished tannins and a long, pure finish.

CHAPTER 9
Hair Trigger

Jordan checked his phone and closed out his computer. The wine was due shortly and he wanted to pick up Simone before everyone got to the winery for unloading. He stood up, grabbing his jacket with an unfamiliar buzz of adrenaline. Unloading a truck might be a lame way to spend an evening, but he was going to see Simone, which took out much of the sting.

"Hey," said Gabe, unexpectedly opening the door to Jordan's office. "The wine's due shortly, right? I told my Dad if anyone wanted to help out for a couple of minutes they should swing by."

"Uh…" Jordan stared at Gabe, still trying to fathom that he was there after hours on a Friday night.

"Truck. Wine. Bruh?" asked Gabe, breaking the question down to the most basic parts.

"Yeah," said Jordan. "Sorry, yeah. Are you staying?" Jordan reached for his clipboard to check the names of the people he'd coerced into helping. "I didn't think I talked to you."

"Yeah," said Gabe, "But I saw Simone's post this morning. Hashtag Amante Life," Gabe made the hashtag sign with his fingers and pulled a band-boy pose that made Jordan chuckle. "It was about the Barolo arriving tonight, so I figured you'd need help. You could have asked me."

"I've asked you before," said Jordan drily. "Seems like George and I ended up unloading last weekend."

Gabe had the decency to look embarrassed. "Yeah," he said. "Sorry. I guess I just didn't realize how much other people were doing until I started seeing all of Simone's posts. I thought you just had some sort of cushy gig where you got to taste wine all the time. I didn't realize how much you actually do."

Jordan tried to formulate a response. "I don't know whether to laugh or be really offended," he said after a moment.

"Probably offended. Dad says I'm clueless," said Gabe, looking glum.

Gabe's father, Santiago, was head of the field hands, and Jordan thought the two, with their wildly different personalities, probably found it hard to connect.

"You're not clueless," said Jordan. "You're smart. But you slack off all the time."

"I don't want to screw anything up," said Gabe. "I figure you guys know more, so I should stay out of it."

"You're never going to learn if you don't show up," said Jordan.

Gabe gestured to himself as if to say, *here I am.*

"Point taken. Well, tonight, you can learn about unloading boxes."

"I already know about that," said Gabe. "But I'm going to do it anyway."

Jordan grinned. "All right, well, I'm going to go pick up Simone. How about you go down to the dock and show me what you know about organizing teams for unloading." He shoved the clipboard at Gabe. "This is who you've got to work with."

"I can do that," said Gabe, looking excited. "Thanks!"

"Thanks for showing up," said Jordan.

"Yeah," said Gabe, flushing. "I... Any time."

Jordan left the winery feeling as if all of the dice that he'd been rolling were coming up sevens. He was going to go pick up the prettiest girl in three counties, and his co-workers were pulling together, and the wine was almost here, and judging was tomorrow and he was going to win. Everything was going to be perfect.

"Hey!" exclaimed Simone, beaming as she and Skipper climbed into the truck.

"Hey!" he replied, and Simone laughed.

"Your evening is going that good too?"

"Yes, it is! What's great about yours?"

"I talked to my aunt. We… well, everything's fine." Simone paused and then looked at him in some confusion. "She's really serious about Mateo. She's thinking about moving here."

"That's great news," said Jordan, feeling like he could almost hear the dice go click, click, click as they tumbled. If Juliet was moving here, that would make it so much easier for Simone to stay.

"She seems really happy," Simone said, although she sounded more cautious.

He pulled into the parking lot just behind Michelle and Graham. The kids waved at him like crazy through the back window, which made Simone laugh. The parking lot was half-full, and Jordan used his employee privileges to pull up to the warehouse.

"I'm going to run into the office real quick and stash my purse," said Simone.

"Hey," said Michelle, walking up with the kids and Graham in tow.

"Can I pet your dog?" asked Mason, staring at Skipper in fascination.

"Yes," said Simone. "In fact, can you do me a favor and hold his leash while I go into the office?" Mason's eyes got huge.

"I'm good with dogs," he said. "I can do that, right, Mom?"

Michelle glanced at Simone. "If it's OK with Simone, then it's OK with me."

"Awesome!" exclaimed Mason as Simone handed over the leash.

Simone grinned. "I'll be back in a minute," she said to Jordan, heading toward the back entrance and the interior courtyard.

"I was promised wine," said Graham, looking at the assembled crowd. "Wine in exchange for box lifting. But jeez, Jordan, I'm not sure you're going to need our help."

"My spotter says the truck just turned off the freeway," said Gabe, coming up. He had the clipboard in one hand and a walkie-talkie in the other.

"Your spotter?" asked Jordan, laughing.

"I sent my cousin up into the loft with binoculars," said Gabe, grinning. "Mateo came in while you were gone. He's in the office. Said he'd be right back. Do you guys want to be in the unload, load, or passing team?" he asked, turning to Michelle and Graham.

"Passing team," said Graham without hesitation. "Teams that pass win every time."

"I'm not sure basketball rules work in wine," said Jordan.

"Basketball rules work everywhere," said Graham confidently, which made Michelle raise her eyebrows skeptically.

"All right," said Gabe. "You're used to yelling at people, so you can go over to George and get trained on being team Captain, and then you can yell at other people until they also know how to pass."

"You're going out with the Team Captain, babe," said Graham, over his shoulder as he followed Gabe toward the back of the loading dock and Michelle laughed.

"Goodness, Jordan," said Michelle, looking around. "Where did all these people come from? We're probably going to be done in about a minute. I think I'm still going to owe you for babysitting!"

"Well, a very smart woman has been telling me to not do everything myself and to embrace my inner boss, so I thought I asked some people to help."

"Well, Simone is definitely right on this one."

"No, that was you, sis."

"Oh," said Michelle, looking touched. "Well... I still think Simone had a hand in this. Caleb said maybe that you two had hit it off. I don't suppose you've considered maybe asking her out?"

"Always pushing," said Jordan, shaking his head.

"I'm looking out for you!" exclaimed Michelle.

"Yeah, well for your information, I did ask her out and we sort of made plans, but we keep getting interrupted by..." He waved at his assembled friends and family.

Michelle cackled in complete unrepentance and Jordan shook his head.

"I'm walking away now. But hey, before I leave, since we will be done early, I thought all the volunteers would like to go bowling in town?"

"Who are you, and what have you done with my baby brother?"

"I'll take that as a yes."

"Yes, of course. The kids will love it. Although, now I've lost my children." She turned around and surveyed the lot.

"Robin headed into the courtyard, probably to read under the heat lamp," said Jordan. "And Mason ran that way to play with Skipper."

"Next thing you know, he's going to want a dog," said Michelle.

"I believe what you mean," said Graham, returning, "is that the next thing you know, we'll be caving and getting a dog."

"That sounds like us," agreed Michelle.

Jordan wasn't paying attention. Across the loading bay, he saw Mateo come in with Simone. She waved, and he waved back.

"Ahem," said Michelle, giving him a significant eyebrow.

"Pushing," said Jordan.

There was a rumble, and the truck from the labeler came into the bay. There was a cheer from the assembled team. The delivery driver didn't look like he was used to receiving a hero's welcome but seemed happy to have it. The palettes were unloaded, and then the teams Gabe had devised formed a chain of hands to unload, pass, and reload the individual crates into the Amante truck.

Santiago Gonzalez, Gabe's father, left the passing chain as the stream of crates began to trickle to a stop. Santiago was shaped like a fire hydrant and definitely just as tough. He ran the field crews with iron, but friendly, fists. Jordan had always admired him.

"Jordan," said Santiago, holding out a hand. Jordan shook it with a smile. Santiago didn't talk much, but when he did, his words were worth listening to. "What did you say to my son? He's being… ambitious."

"Nothing," said Jordan. "This is all him."

They watched as Gabe dropped his clipboard to pitch in himself. Simone hovered at the edge of the line, seeming torn between working and trying to take pictures.

"Do we think he just wanted into the pictures?" asked Santiago surveying the scene.

"No, we think he really wanted to help," said Jordan, laughing. "And *also* into the pictures."

Santiago laughed, too, and gave Jordan a light punch on the arm. "I'll still take it. Good luck at the Classic tomorrow."

"Thanks," said Jordan. "I hope we don't need any luck, but thanks."

Santiago nodded and strode away. Across the loading bay, Mateo laughingly ordered Simone to just take pictures as Jordan approached them.

"I came to help, though," she protested.

"You can drive the truck down to the lower lot and park it

for the morning. That can be your help," said Mateo, chuckling.

Jordan turned to look at the truck with a frown. "That's a big truck, and the slope on the lot can be tricky in the dark. I think we should just get one of the guys with a proper commercial license," said Jordan.

"I have a CDL," said Simone. "I got it for the motorhome."

"Is there anything you can't do?" demanded Jordan.

"Um… Omelets and pancakes."

"You have something against breakfast?" asked Mateo.

"No. I just can't flip anything to save my life," said Simone. "They always come out kind of a scrambled mess. Which is OK for omelets but ruins the effect on pancakes."

"Jordan makes great pancakes," said Mateo. "I once watched him do a triple flip three feet above his head at the Elks Club fundraiser."

"Have you been talking to my sister?" asked Jordan, looking at Mateo skeptically.

"No, but I did run into your mother last week," said Mateo, with an impish twinkle in his eye.

"Uh-huh," said Jordan. "You two are coming for bowling, right?"

"Yeah," said Mateo, "I'm going to stop and…" he trailed off, his eyes swiveling toward Simone.

Simone giggled gleefully. "Pick up my aunt. Yes. We thought you might want to do that."

Mateo looked sheepish. "We were going to tell you."

"I talked to her about it earlier. Do you want me to text her and warn her that she's about to go bowling?"

"I'll just go call her," said Mateo. "Meet you over there?"

"Yeah," said Jordan.

"Can I ride with you to the bowling alley?" asked Simone as Mateo left.

"Of course," said Jordan. Simone took a step closer, and Jordan found he was holding his breath.

"Hey," said Michelle, coming around the corner. "We're done loading. I still can't believe it. Have you seen Mason? Graham said he saw him playing in the lower lot with Skipper?"

Simone took a rapid step backward, and Jordan let out his breath.

"I'm about to move the truck to the back lot, so I'll walk him and Skipper back," said Simone.

"Thanks," said Michelle.

Simone flashed a smile at Jordan over her shoulder before heading for the truck.

"Michelle!" said Jordan, glaring at his sister. "You're timing is…"

Michelle glanced at Simone and then back at Jordan and chuckled. "Consider it payback for all the times you kept wandering in on me and Bill Iverson."

"That was like tenth grade," said Jordan sourly, which made Michelle laugh harder.

Simone

As Simone started the heavy engine of the truck and was surprised that the loud sound felt steadying. Maybe she was missing Matilda more than she thought. She took a deep breath and looked around the cab, familiarizing herself with the controls. She eased the truck down the winding drive to the lower parking lot, perched directly above the hill down into town. In the morning they would finish loading up all the equipment for the event and take everything into Luckless.

She drove cautiously, listening for the sound of any sliding in the rear of the truck, but everything seemed stable. As she rounded the corner into the lot she spotted Mason and Skipper playing some form of tag fetch with an old wine barrel stave. She slowed to a crawl and parked the truck, carefully setting the emergency brake, and climbed down from the cab.

"Hi," said Mason, waving as Simone reached the ground. Skipper took the opportunity to snatch the stick from Mason's hand and came bounding toward Simone, utter glee in his eye. Simone reached for him, but he dodged and bounced up into the truck. He spun in the driver's seat to see them, the stave in his mouth, lifting it high as if to proclaim victory.

"Hey!" exclaimed Mason, reaching for the stave.

"No," said Simone, laughing. "No playing around in cars. Too dangerous."

"But he's got the stick!" protested Mason.

"I'll get it back in a minute," said Simone. "Just give me a chance to lock up."

She went to the back of the truck, lifted the rolling door, and checked the interior. The wine was all in place, and everything looked fine. She rolled the door closed with a rattle of ball bearings and a reassuring clunk and then used the padlock to secure the door. She patted the door and went back to the front of the truck.

Mason was holding Skipper and the stick and looking smug. She sensed that Skipper had allowed himself to be outwitted.

"Everything good to go?" asked George, coming down the hill with Michelle and Graham in tow.

"I just locked up," said Simone.

"Time to give the dog back, pumpkin bread," said Michelle.

"Oh, OK," said Mason, looking as though she'd asked him to give away all his Halloween candy.

"Hurry up and get in the car, Mase," said Graham. "We're all going bowling with Uncle Jordan."

"Bowling? Yes!" Mason shoved Skipper at Simone and took off at a sprint.

"I see where we are in the rankings, Skipper," said Simone with a laugh.

"Pretty sure everything comes after Uncle Jordan," said Graham. "I swear he must have just fed them ice cream every day we were gone."

"Bribery is the babysitter's friend," said Simone knowingly. She put Skipper down and handed the truck keys to George.

"Thanks," said George. "You want to drive it tomorrow? I've got to be over at the event early, and Mateo hates driving this thing."

"Sure," said Simone. "Whatever needs to be done."

"Great," said George, nodding. "I'll leave the keys in the office. Jordan said to meet him at his truck, and then everyone's meeting at the bowling alley."

Simone met Jordan at his truck, and she was on his team for bowling and when he ordered fries, he let her eat half without complaining. Simone tried not to totally embarrass herself, but she found that she kept staring at Jordan. She hadn't felt anything like this since she had been a teenager. And even then, those high school crushes couldn't hold a candle to the tumbling mix of emotions she felt about Jordan. She knew the rest of the Amante employees, and Michelle noticed. But nobody said anything. Which Simone thought was very kind. With some coaching from Jordan, Simone bowled a perfect strike and decided that Luckless was utterly misnamed—because she felt so lucky. Everything was perfect.

Mateo's phone rang in his jacket, and he fumbled through his pockets, looking for it.

"Mom," said Robin, leaning down to her mother's purse, "I think your phone's ringing."

Then Jordan's phone rang, and he pulled it out of his back pocket, frowning at the number.

"Shoot," said Mateo, finally finding his phone just as it quit ringing.

"This is Jordan Ryan," he said, using what Simone thought of as his professional voice. The smile slipped off his face as he listened to whoever was on the other end of the phone call. "It's where?" He was stripped off his shoes as he talked, slamming them on the counter and snapping his fingers at the teenager behind the desk. "I'll be there as soon as I can."

Simone and the assembled Amante group watched in disbelief as he snatched his shoes from the teenager but ran out of the bowling alley still in his stocking feet.

"That was the Sheriff's department," said Mateo, listening to his messages.

"Mine too," said Michelle.

"They say our truck is overturned on the road," said Mateo, looking ill.

"They need a tow truck," said Michelle.

Simone could feel everyone turn to look at her. "I don't understand," said Simone, looking at the group. "What does that mean?"

"I think we'd better go see what's happened," said Mateo, clearing his throat.

Simone looked at Juliette. "I'll drive you," said Juliette. "I've got the rental. Mateo, you should hurry after Jordan."

He nodded and hurried out of the bowling alley. The rest of the party split up, and Juliette and Simone eventually managed to get onto the road out of town. As they swung onto the winery approach road, she saw Jordan and Mateo standing at the base of the hill near the fountain, the scene illuminated by the flashing red and blue lights of two police cars. They appeared to be looking at some vehicle with just the underside in view – then it dawned on her. It was the delivery truck that they'd just loaded on its side.

"No, no, no, no!" gasped Simone, her fingers gripping into the dash of the car.

Juliette slowed to a stop, and Simone leaped out. She ran to the truck. It was completely tipped over. The frame was clearly bent. The padlock had popped on the back door, and even in the dark, she could see wine and broken glass spilling out.

"What happened?"

Jordan slowly turned around with a look of stone on his face. "It looks like someone didn't set the emergency brake."

"The emergency brake?

"You know, the thing that keeps the truck from sliding down the hill and breaking every bottle of Barolo."

The blue lights gave Jordan's face strange angles, making him seem alien.

"Every bottle?" she whispered.

"Yes," he said, his tone harsh and grating. "Every bottle. Simone. How could you not set the emergency brake?"

"But I did. I always do."

He gestured angrily at the mess on the grass.

"I thought I did," she protested, suddenly unsure. "I'm sorry!"

"I guess if I wanted it done right, I should have done it myself," snapped Jordan, pivoting away from her.

"Jordan, wait!" She grabbed at his sleeve, tugging on it.

Jordan wheeled and, with a coldness that she'd never seen, said, "Don't." He backed away from her and then ran. Moments later, she heard his truck start up and roar up the hill to the winery.

Simone felt frozen in place. In her mind, she ran through the events of the evening. She had set the emergency brake. Hadn't she? Mateo touched her arm, and she winced at the unexpected touch.

"Mateo, I don't understand. I remember setting the emergency brake. I really do. I can't believe this happened. I swear, I remember setting it... maybe I didn't do it all the way?"

Mateo sighed and rubbed his face. "It's an old truck, and it's a steep grade. It may have slipped on its own. We should have left it parked at the warehouse. It's not your fault. I can try to call the labeler in the morning. Maybe there's something they can do. Some wine they can send down."

"It's Saturday," said George, staring at the truck as if he couldn't look away. "They won't be open."

"I can't come in," said Simone. "I broke all the wine."

Mateo sighed again. "We'll think of something in the morning. There has to be something we can do. Things will look better when you come in tomorrow."

"I don't think I should do that," whispered Simone. "I don't think Jordan wants me here."

"No," said Mateo firmly. "Simone, please stay. Amante needs you, and Jordan and I do too. Just give him some time, and he will come around."

"I don't think so, Mateo," said Simone, a tear slipping down her face. "I may have broken more than just wine bottles."

CHAPTER 10
In Deep

Simone

Caleb was tactfully quiet and sympathetically trying to feed her pastries. Which was sweet. But a donut was no croissant. In matters of heartbreak, the ratio of sugar to fat was crucial, and cinnamon sugar sprinkles could not be substituted for buttery flakiness.

Not that she wanted to eat either of them. What was the point of eating? Or sleeping? She hadn't done that either. Her eyes felt gritty like she face-planted into the sandman's bag, but hadn't gotten any more than sand for her trouble.

Her aunt had poked her head in at some point in the morning to say that she was going down to the event. Unless Simone didn't want her to go and then she wouldn't go. Should she stay? Simone had said to go. There hadn't been any point in hogging her aunt's time or keeping her away from Mateo. It wasn't Juliette's fault that Simone was a screw-up.

The worst part was that she couldn't fix it. This felt like when her Dad had died. There was no changing that either. No bargaining it away. No amount of railing against it would make a difference. Like the spinning of the globe, it just kept coming, sweeping everything before it.

Death, broken wine bottles, and broken hearts.

No changes.

No substitutions.

"Do you want something other than a donut?" asked Caleb. "We can swap it out for a Danish?" He held up the box of pastries. "Ooh. Or a cinnamon roll."

"I wish I had a croissant," said Simone sadly.

"Mmm, one of the many French contributions to bettering life on this planet," agreed Caleb. "Sadly, not included in my selection from the bakery."

The clouds parted outside the window and struck the donut on her plate with a ray of sunshine.

"French substitutes," said Simone, bolting upright and knocking over her chair. "I…" She looked at Caleb in panic. "What time is it?"

"About 9:30," said Caleb, checking the microwave.

"We can still make it! Skipper! I have to go!"

"Make what?" asked Caleb, looking perplexed.

"The contest! We can still get in. Skipper!" She looked around, and Skipper was already at her feet.

"Do you need the car?" asked Caleb, handing her a leash.

"There's no time to park! I have to go."

"Well, I'm not sure…" began Caleb, but Simone was already running out of the house.

"Thank you!" she yelled over her shoulder.

She dashed down the block, heading for the town square. The pedestrians became more frequent as she got closer to the event. Dodging left and right, she finally ducked under the ropes and into the vendor-designated area behind the tents. Each tent had the winery's name on a paper sign blue-taped to the back entrance. She slowed to a speed walk, looking for Amante. She saw the distinctive A shape and broke back into a run. Bursting through the vinyl flaps, she spun around as Skipper, tied to her belt, kept going, pivoting to the left to jump on Gabe.

Gabe managed to catch Skipper and not drop the wine he was in the middle of opening. "Simone?"

"I need Mateo! Where is he?"

"Out front, shaking hands and kissing babies or whatever."

"Hey Simone," said George, coming into the tent with an empty tray. "What's going on?"

"I need Mateo. I have an idea about how we can enter wine for the contest!"

George and Gabe exchanged glances.

"We can't get to the labeler and back in time," said George. "Gabe and I already talked about it."

"No, it's a different wine. Can you just get him for me? I look like crap. I can't go out there."

"Yeah," said Gabe, looking at George for permission. "I'll go."

Gabe slipped out of the tent and returned with Mateo in tow a few minutes later.

"You have an idea?" Mateo asked, a frown creasing his forehead.

"Jordan's wine," said Simone. "You tasted it, right? You know it's brilliant. You need to enter that."

"What wine?" asked George, looking from Simone to Mateo and back. "Jordan has another wine?"

"We can't," protested Mateo.

"Why not?" demanded Simone. "It's your grapes, it's your winemaker. It's Amante wine."

"Because…" Mateo began.

"We have other wine?" demanded George. "Where? How? Why are we not getting it right now?"

"We can't," said Mateo.

"If Jordan has another top-quality wine," said George. "We need to be putting it in a bottle right now. There's barely a half-hour until the judging. We can still enter!"

"We can't!" said Mateo.

"Why not?" George bellowed, throwing up his arms in frustration.

"It's French!" Mateo yelled back.

"And I'm Mexican," said Gabe. "And George is Hungarian. And Laureen is Scots-Irish. This is America. Didn't we fight a whole war so that we could do things differently?"

Mateo looked at Gabe and then at George and Simone. "My grandfather is going to start spinning in his grave."

"He'll stop if you win," said Simone. "But we can't win if we don't enter. We're running out of time."

"I can help with that," said Juliette, and everyone swung around to look at the tent entrance. Juliette was standing there with her straw hat dangling from her fingertips. "Or at least Linda and I can. The mayor is set to make a speech prior to the contest. I think a few quick words in Tricia's ear might make *her* words go a little slower come speech time."

Mateo ran his hand through his hair. "I was supposed to speak too."

"I can help Simone," said George quickly. "You can stay here and stall. What do we have to do?"

"The wine is in a cask in Jordan's bat cave," said Simone. "We need to get it in bottles and then get some labels together. I can do that bit at the office. I've got a template for the Amante standard labels. I just need a name. What are we calling it?"

"How about *Prendres des Risques*?" suggested Juliette, amusement lacing her town. "It's French for *taking risks*."

"May the ancestors forgive me," said Mateo, shaking his head. "Well, don't just stand there—go! We're running out of time!"

Juliette

"This is going to work," said Mateo as he signed the submission form. "We're just going to throw out three years worth of work and put it all on Jordan." His face looked grim.

"You've spent the last three days telling me Jordan is brilliant," said Juliette.

"Jordan *is* brilliant. But this wine… It's his baby. He's already crushed about the Barolo. If this doesn't at least medal, I'm worried he'll think the failure is all on him."

"Do you believe in the wine?" asked Juliette.

Mateo laughed. "Of course. Jordan came out of school understanding grapes in a way that it took me twenty years to figure out. But it's a risk. I just…" He trailed off and then looked at Juliette. "I've never been good at risks," he said sadly. "I just keep to the same paths. Jordan keeps pushing me to try new things, and I want to, but then I go back to the same old ways."

Juliette took his hand and squeezed it. "It's never too late to try a new path."

"You're right," he said, squeezing back. "And I think—no, I know—I need to. I just really didn't think I'd be doing it today with a French Wine."

Juliette laughed. "All right, you go wait for George and Simone. I'm going to go have a word with Linda."

"Good luck," he said, kissing her on the cheek.

"You too," she said and slipped out of the tent.

She found Linda near the Price Mansion, wearing a headset and directing an endless stream of people looking for answers.

"Juliette, hi!" said Linda. "Talk to Rob about the water connection."

"What?" asked Juliette, puzzled. Linda pointed at her headset.

"Yeah, you're clear to move those out. We're going to do opening speeches on the judging in fifteen minutes." Linda paused, appearing to listen, and then nodded. "Great. I'm going offline for a few minutes. Direct your questions to Stacy." Linda pulled her headset down and took a deep breath. "Hey Juliette," she said, leaning in for a hug. "It's so good to see you!"

"You may not think so in a minute," said Juliette. "I'm about to ask for a favor."

"Intriguing! Now I'm dying to know. What's up?"

"I need to delay the start of judging," said Juliette. "Is there any way we can stall?"

"How long do you need?" asked Linda, frowning.

"A half-hour maybe?" suggested Juliette, trying to get the most time. Linda made a face.

"I can probably delay an easy five to ten minutes before starting the speeches. I'll just hide Tricia's hair spray." Juliette laughed involuntarily, and Linda tried not to smile. "But I don't think I can delay getting everyone up on stage longer than that."

"Get us the ten minutes, and then maybe… I was wondering if we couldn't convince Tricia to make her speech a bit longer?"

"Us?" asked Linda, scrutinizing Juliette. "You're Team Amante now?"

"I am," said Juliette. "And the team needs time to get their bottles to the judging table. There was a catastrophic incident last night."

Linda grimaced. "I don't like the sound of catastrophic. All right, I'll have a word with Tricia. She's good at doing the proud mayor bit. This will give her the chance to roll out her history of the town speech. But after this is all over I expect to hear all the details about everything."

"Done," agreed Juliette.

"*Everything*," said Linda, pointing at Juliette and stressing the word.

"Yes, we're dating," said Juliette with a sigh. Linda grinned.

"Great. Go stand by the fountain and give me the high sign when you've got your team in place. And meet me next Thursday at Basic Biscuit for brunch."

"I'll be there," said Juliette, smiling.

Thirty minutes later, Juliette stood on the edge of the fountain and tried to keep an eye out for Simone. Mateo had already gone through his welcoming bit. He'd done as many old man pauses as he could and generally drug his feet, but the Mayor's final speech had arrived all too quickly. Juliette scanned the crowd again and, with relief, saw Simone coming through the crowd.

Simone and Skipper edged through the crowd, and Juliette tried to make a *what's going on* face. Simone gave her a thumbs up, and Juliette turned back to look at the stage and gave Linda a nod. Linda turned and gave Tricia on stage at the podium a subtle thumbs up.

"And that is how the town came to be," said Tricia, her voice picking up speed. "Which just goes to show that while luck may be all when it comes to gold mining, perseverance, and fortitude are more useful when building a town. Thank you all for coming out today! Now, let's get to the wine!"

The assembled crowd gave a whole-hearted cheer, and everyone began to disperse.

"You got the wine in?" whispered Juliette, and Simone nodded.

"Submission form is in. The wine got wrapped and handed off. We're in the contest."

"Did you tell Jordan what you were doing?" asked Juliette.

"We couldn't find him," said Simone, looking glassy-eyed. "George called him, but he didn't pick up."

"Well, I guess you can tell him when you see him. He has to turn up eventually."

"No," said Simone. "I'm not going to stay."

"Simone, you have to stay."

"No," she said, shaking her head. "I can't. I just can't. I really screwed up everything for Jordan and the winery."

"You know Mateo has forgiven you, right?" demanded Juliette.

"Yes, but Jordan hasn't. I just can't stay."

"Not even for the judging?"

"I'll read about it online. George was having a heart attack trying to get it in the bottles, but it's the judging that gives me a panic attack. I think I'm too chicken to stay. This is my best shot at fixing my screw-up, but... Even if the wine wins, I don't think it's enough. Anyway, Michelle says Matilda is fixed, so I'm going to head over to the garage and then head for Colorado."

"What's in Colorado?" demanded Juliette. "You don't need to go back!"

"I know there's not much left for me there," said Simone, "but there is nothing left for me here." Her eyes welled up with tears, and Juliette hugged her tightly.

"I will always be here for you," she promised fiercely.

"Thanks," said Simone, hugging her back. "Maybe I'm making too much of this, but all I know is that I just can't face waking up tomorrow knowing that I'm not going back to... the winery."

"I'm so sorry," said Juliette, feeling her own eyes well up.

"Yeah," said Simone. "Me too." She gave a sniff and put her chin up. "But I will be all right. Because a Laurent can do anything."

"That's right," said Juliette, smiling. "We can. But we can also call our aunt when we get to the next stop and check-in."

Simone laughed sheepishly. "Yeah, all right. I'll call tonight."

"I'll tell you how everything goes," said Juliette, gesturing to the judging tent, but she meant with Jordan.

"Thanks," said Simone, and hugged her again.

Juliette watched Skipper and Simone go and tried to devise a way to convince her to stay.

"Is Simone leaving?" demanded Mateo, striding up.

Juliette nodded, unwilling to trust her voice.

"She can't," said Mateo, sounding distressed. "We've got to be able to fix this. I will talk to Jordan. I tried to call him this morning, but he didn't pick up."

"Simone said George called him too with the same result. I couldn't convince her to stay," said Juliette sadly. "I don't know what else to do."

CHAPTER 11
New Resolutions

Jordan woke up with a groan and frightened a bird that had landed on the empty wine bottle in the passenger seat. Jordan opened the car door of the Spider and fell out onto the dirt of the grape field. He leaned against the car door and stared out at the rows of grapes. He'd drunk at least three bottles, and his head felt like it had been four.

"Jordan?" asked a friendly voice and he looked up at Santiago Gonzalez standing by the rear of the car.

"Hey, Santiago," he said without bothering to get up.

"Is everything…" Santiago looked over the edge of the car at the wine bottles. "OK?"

"No," said Jordan. "I think I'm in love with a girl who just ruined our chances of winning at the Classic. Which means that literally years of our lives just got wiped out."

"Gabe told me about the truck," said Santiago, nodding. "But that was just the wine for the Classic, right? The rest that was going to be for sale is still at the labeler, isn't it?"

"Yeah, but the point was to win so we could market it the heck out of it," said Jordan. "Without a win, it's just another Amante wine."

Santiago scratched his head. "Well, that's not exactly nothing. And also, can we perhaps talk about the girl?"

"What's the point?" asked Jordan, picking up a wine bottle that had fallen out with him and throwing it into the field. "She's leaving town."

Santiago reached over and flicked him in the head.

"Hey!" Jordan looked up at Santiago in shock, putting his hand up to his stinging ear.

"Yes," said Santiago. "Hey! You're in love! Why are you sitting here like an idiot?"

Jordan stared at Santiago, trying to formulate words.

"She said she was sorry, and I yelled at her," he said. Santiago gave him a look that said that further flicking might be imminent. "I can't... She's leaving..."

"Only if you don't go get her," said Santiago. "Wine is wine. It's wonderful stuff, but it's not someone who holds you at the end of the night. Get your priorities straight, son."

Santiago shook his head and walked off.

Jordan stared out at the fields. Then he stood up and dusted himself off.

Twenty minutes later, Jordan knocked on the front door of Sir Barkington's Bed and Breakfast for dogs and their people and only then remembered to run his hand through his hair and try to tuck in his shirt.

"Jordan Ryan!" exclaimed Caleb, opening the door. "What on earth are you doing here?"

"I need to talk to Simone," said Jordan, abandoning the shirt effort halfway through.

"You can't," said Caleb simply.

"No," said Jordan. "You don't understand. It's just wine. I freaked out because of the Classic, but it's just wine. I can make more wine. I really..." He stumbled to a stop and looked at Caleb in desperation. "I need Simone."

"I was not questioning the actual need," said Caleb. "I'm telling you that you can't because she's not here. She was pretending to eat breakfast this morning, stood up and declared she had an idea to get you back in the Classic and ran out of the house with Skipper."

"What idea?" asked Jordan, perplexed.

"I don't know," said Caleb. "I was assuming she was with you down at the event."

"No," said Jordan. "I didn't go. I fell asleep in my car and came straight here when I woke up."

"Well, didn't anyone call you?"

Jordan fished in his pocket for his phone and pushed the home button a few times, but nothing happened. "It's dead," he said. "What time is it?"

"Nearly one, I think," said Caleb. "But Jordan, Simone packed her things last night. She said she was leaving today as soon as Michelle got the motorhome fixed."

"No, the judging's not over," said Jordan. "If she figured out how to get us into the competition, then she can't have left yet. There's still time."

"Well, then you'd better get down to the event," said Caleb. "And then text me when you get there because I'm dying to know what happened."

"Right," said Jordan, turning around. "Right," he said, turning around the other way.

"Car keys. Then that way," said Caleb, pointing at the car,

"Right," said Jordan for the third time and ran toward the Spider.

Jordan spent several road rage-filled minutes trying to find a parking spot before managing to wedge the Spider into a tiny spot in the vendor lot and then ran toward the event. He found the tent and booth for Amante, but it was roped closed with a sign that read: AT THE JUDGING.

Reluctantly, he headed for the main stage. The other winemakers were all standing on stage wearing medals and hoisting their wine bottles and Jordan tried to focus on finding Simone and any of his co-workers. He didn't want to feel the bitter wash of defeat to sour what he had to say to Simone.

The head judge approached the microphone carrying the Classic Cup, and Jordan wished he could somehow have missed this part entirely.

"And the winner of the Decanter Classic International Cup for Best in Show with a Chardonnay: *Prendres des Risques* from the Amante winery."

There was a roar of approval from the crowd, and Jordan swayed on his feet. Everything was so loud that he thought he'd gone deaf. Up on stage, Mateo was hoisting the cup and beaming.

"*Prendres des Risques*, for those who don't speak French," said Mateo into the mic, "can be translated as *taking risks*. I encourage all of you to take more risks. We only get one life. We should all be lucky enough to find people who make us more loving, more fearless, and more than the sum of our parts. I have that with my family at Amante, and I thank each and every one of them, but particularly Jordan Ryan, who makes wine that I can now truly describe as some of the best in the world."

There was another cheer from the crowd, and someone reached over and shook his hand and thumped him on the back. Jordan staggered and couldn't stop himself from being pushed toward the stage and the rest of the Amante employees.

George hugged him. Gabe was jumping up and down and Mateo looked like he was floating on air. Jordan saw Juliette beaming as if her face was nothing but smile. But as hard as he looked, he didn't see Simone.

"Jordan!"

He turned toward the female voice that was calling his name and saw with disappointment that it was Michelle and their mother.

"Jordan!" yelled Cynthia over the noise of the crowd. "We need to talk!" She had Mason in tow, and when the boy saw Jordan, he hid behind Cynthia.

"What's the matter?" asked Jordan, reaching for Mason. He didn't know what was going on, but Mason looked like he desperately needed a hug.

"It's OK, pumpkin," said Cynthia. "Uncle Jordan won't yell at you, I promise." She shot Jordan a glare that said he'd better not yell at her grandchild, or there would be severe consequences.

"Mom, what's going on?" demanded Michelle, trying to pry Mason away from his grandmother. "Why would Jordan yell at Mason?"

"I broke your wine," wailed Mason, shoving off Cynthia to hide his face in Michelle's stomach.

Jordan looked at both Michelle and Cynthia in confusion.

"He was playing with Skipper and went into the truck and knocked the emergency brake off," said Cynthia, patting her grandson's back, her eyes full of anxiety and apology.

Jordan closed his eyes, and when he opened them again, he started to laugh. Michelle glared at him, and he managed to pull himself together.

"Mason," he tried to peel Mason away from Michelle. "Mason, buddy. It's OK. It was an accident." He finally got his nephew turned around and knelt down to hug him. "It's OK. I know you didn't mean to."

Mason hugged him tightly.

"What's going on?" asked Mateo, coming over, still carrying the cup.

"Simone didn't crash the truck," said Cynthia. "It was Mason and Skipper. They knocked the emergency brake off. I tried to call Jordan, but it went straight to voicemail." She paused to glare at Jordan for his poor phone habits. "So we came to find you."

"It's OK," said Jordan, standing and picking up Mason as he did. "I just have to find Simone. She'll be really relieved to know. Where is she?" he asked, turning to Mateo.

Mateo's face seemed frozen. "She left," he said.

"No," said Jordan, looking around the event as if she would suddenly appear. "No, the event's not over. I got here in time."

"She said she couldn't stand to see the judging," said Juliette.

"You're squishing me, Uncle Jordan," said Mason.

"Sorry, bud," said Jordan, setting Mason down. He felt like he was going to throw up.

"She said she'd call me tonight," offered Juliette, looking like she knew it was cold comfort. "Maybe we can get her to come back."

Jordan felt unsteady on his feet. He'd been so certain he could fix everything if he got to the event on time. Now, he felt like the bottom had dropped out. Mateo put an arm around him, and Jordan leaned on him because he wasn't sure he could stand up any longer.

"Or maybe you should get in your car and go get her," said Michelle. Everyone turned to look at Michelle as if she'd just suggested he grow wings and fly. "You won't have to drive very far. She's probably going to be breaking down at any minute."

"What?" asked Jordan.

"She's the only girl who's ever had you turning in circles. I figured you just needed a little more time, so I may have… removed a few pieces when she came by to get the motorhome today. It was not an ethical decision from the mechanic's point of view, but I figured it was the least I could do as a big sister."

"That's my girl," said Cynthia smugly.

"I have to go," said Jordan.

"Yes," agreed Mateo.

"Like now," said Jordan.

"Yes," said Michelle.

"Good luck," said Juliette, grinning. "But I don't think you'll need it."

"I..." Jordan stared at his friends and family. "Bye," he said and took off running for his car.

Simone

Matilda clunked to a halt next to the Luckless fountain, and Simone slowly climbed out and stared at the grape fields and the winery in the distance. Then she folded down the steps into the living portion and sat down on them. Skipper snuffled around her feet.

"I can't, Skipper," she said. "I just can't. I know Laurents can do anything, but I think maybe Grandpa was talking about a different Laurent." Tears began to slide down her face, and she picked up Skipper and hugged him.

There was the sound of a motor in the distance, and then it got closer and came to a halt in front of the fountain. Simone leaned forward to see around Matilda's bumper and saw with surprise that it was Jordan in his convertible. Jordan vaulted over the side of his car without bothering to open the door. He ran to the driver's door on the other side of the motorhome. She heard the door open and then slam shut.

"Simone!" He sounded panicked.

"Over here," she called weakly.

He came dashing around Matilda and stood in front of Simone, breathing heavily. His shirt was half-untucked, and his hair was sticking up on one side like he'd slept on it. Simone didn't know what to say.

"You have to come home," he blurted out.

Simone stared at Jordan. Her world had shattered into a thousand pieces, just like the wine bottles and here was Jordan running in to fix it. Because that's what Jordan did. He made everything better.

"I don't have a home," said Simone.

"Yes, you do," he said. "It's here. It's here in Luckless. Where we want you. Where *I* want you."

"You said…" began Simone.

"I say a lot of stupid things," said Jordan. "If you hold all of them against me, we're never going to get anywhere. You didn't crash the truck, and even if you had it doesn't matter. It was a mistake and mistakes happen. I can make more wine. I can't make another you."

Skipper pushed off her lap and trotted toward Jordan. Then the dog stopped, staring back at Simone as if to say *why aren't you coming?* Simone stood up feeling shaky and uncertain.

"Jordan, it's too late. You don't want…"

"I don't want what? Someone who is beautiful and talented and caring and hard-working and has an adorable dog and motorhome? Because I'm pretty sure I do."

Simone took a step closer and stared up into Jordan's blue eyes. She wanted this to be real. She wanted Jordan and Luckless and everything that went with it more than anything. But there was one thing that maybe Jordan wouldn't want. And there wasn't going to be any way to hide it.

"You should probably know," she said, "I entered your *sur lie* wine into the Classic. George and I put it in bottles. We called *Prendres des Risques,* and Mateo entered it into the Classic for Amante."

"Uh-huh," he said, reaching out and pulling her close to him. "And you should probably know that we won."

Then he kissed her, and the world melted away until the only stable thing in the entire universe was him and his arms around her.

After a long moment, he pulled back. Simone looked up at him, dazed. "What do you mean *we won*?"

"We won," said Jordan. "We won the Classic International Cup by *Prendres des Risques*. We won because of you."

Simone tried to make thoughts and words happen, but she couldn't, so she kissed him instead.

PART 4:

A Celebration...
With French-Style
Sparkling Wine

We recommend pairing this section with a sparkling wine. As the legendary French monk Dom Pérignon, who serendipitously discovered champagne, is said to have exclaimed, 'I am tasting the stars!' Indeed, nothing captures the spirit of celebration quite like a taste of the stars, a moment where every bubble feels like a celestial dance in your glass.

Our pick the *2022 The Muse Sparkling from Siren Song.*

TASTING NOTES: You'll find beautifully delicate bubbles alongside notes of honeysuckle, lemon, and the first peach of the season, followed by a long, elegant finish.

CHAPTER 12
Happily Ever After

Simone

Simone held Jordan's hand and watched Juliette and Mateo at the bridal table as half of Luckless laughed and toasted in the Amante Winery central courtyard. Seven months in Luckless had flown past. Juliette hadn't even finished selling her condo yet, but neither she or Mateo had wanted to wait to start their second chance at love. Above them, giant globe lanterns lit the night sky like tiny moons brought down within wishing distance. The tables were awash in flowers and bottles of wine. Juliette was a vision in cream lace, and Mateo was debonair in a gray suit. Simone leaned into Jordan's shoulder and tried not to cry again. Jordan shifted to put an arm around her shoulders.

"I knew I didn't pack enough tissues," he said, patting his pockets.

"They look so happy," said Simone, dabbing her eyes.

"They are so happy," said Jordan, squeezing her tightly.

"I really do need to stop crying," she said. "I cried this morning when Juliette and I buried Dad's ashes in the grape fields, and I cried all through the ceremony, and given half a chance, I'm going to just turn into a fountain all over again."

"The prettiest fountain in the place," said Jordan, and Simone laughed.

"I think you might be prejudiced," she said.

"Maybe," he said, not sounding in the least convinced. "You know there might be a tissue in the pocket closest to you if you want to reach in."

"You just don't want to move your arm," said Simone, reaching into the pocket of his suit jacket.

"Nope, I really don't," he said, leaving his arm around her shoulders.

She felt in his pocket and found a small box instead of the soft pack of tissues that she'd expected. She pulled it out and stared at it in puzzlement. It was small and velvety, like a jewelry box.

"What's this?"

"That is yours," said Jordan. Then he cleared his throat, and she looked up at him. He looked nervous. "If you want it."

She looked at the box again and then back up at Jordan. Then she opened the box and stared at the diamond ring inside.

"Jordan Ryan," she said, blinking rapidly, "didn't I just say that I didn't want to cry again?"

"I actually do have more tissues in my other pocket," he said.

"I love you," she said, staring up at him in disbelief.

"So… is that a yes?" he asked.

"Oh! Yes! Yes, that was a yes!"

He laughed and pulled her in tight for a kiss. There was a flash of light, and Simone looked around in surprise as Gabe took their picture.

"She said yes!" Gabe yelled, turning back to the guests, and there was a loud cheer from the entire party. Juliette clapped her hands and looked elated.

"A toast!" exclaimed Mateo, standing up and picking up his glass. "To Simone and Jordan! *Propino tibi!*"

"You know," said Jordan, looking at the assembled friends and family, "this may be the town of Luckless, but right now, I think I'm the luckiest man alive."

"We're both lucky," said Simone, and under the silver moon and the golden lights and with the scent of grapes in the air, Jordan leaned down and kissed her.

WANT MORE?
Try...

Love & Treasure

Chase Regard is captain of the nearly-historically-accurate pirate ship Cupid's Revenge, a pirate-themed restaurant and dinner show, and the mountain of debt that came with both. But Chase has an ace up his sleeve: his ancestor left a heap of treasure somewhere on the coast near Ashville, Oregon. All Chase needs to find it is the help of the red-headed, fiery, and occasionally forgetful, academic Dr. Jenna Mackenzie, the director of the Ashville Museum. But when Chase and Jenna team up they must face the town's history-buff bully, accusations of theft, and an oncoming storm before they find out that X marks the spot for love and treasure.

READ THE SNEAK PEEK...

Chapter 1

Jenna

Dr. Jenna Mackenzie was a thirty-year-old red-head who held degrees in museum management and art history. She was a serious researcher, the director of the Ashville museum, and completely alone in the museum's research library. Which was why Jenna was sliding along the shelves on the rolling ladder like a red Corvette on a Hot Wheels track.

Jenna checked the book in her hand. *North American Piracy of the Nineteenth Century* needed be shelved all the way at the end of book cases. The ornate antique wooden shelves looked like something out of a fairy tale and, ten feet above the ground, Jenna felt a twinge of guilt as she braced her foot against the shelf full botanical books with the hand tinted art plates. Possibly ladder racing in an antique library was not a recommended preservation technique? On the other hand, she was absolutely certain that if she pushed hard enough she could make the ladder slide all the way to the end of the line.

The library was one of the jewels of the Ashville Museums facilities. A beautifully preserved 1820s mansion and library constructed from native Oregon fir and granite drew history buffs from across three states to the tiny town to marvel at the Victorian edifice. Originally the home of the town founder William Ash, the library featured the finest craftsmanship, up to and including the broad double doors at the far end of shelves Jenna was aiming for. She paused and did a quick check on those very doors.

They were securely shut.

Jenna took a firm grip on her book and the ladder and braced her foot. She was about to break her own distance record. Jenna counted: one, two, annnnnnd three. With a hard kick she shoved off. The ladder sailed along the recently polished brass pole mounted to the wall, seeming to pick up speed as she went. As she reached the half-way point Jenna realized two things: one, the door to the library was opening, and two, she was not slowing down.

The ladder reached the brass stopper with a hard whack and Jenna's grip jerked free, sending her flying through the air straight at the newest visitor to the library—an utterly delectable dark-haired man in a pea coat and three days-worth of stubble.

Chase

Chase Regard was thirty-five, on his third career, and generally believed that nothing in life was worth doing if you weren't having fun doing it. At the moment he was having a great deal of fun because the gods had seen fit to drop a woman from the sky and straight into his arms. He was not at all sure what he'd done to deserve a curvaceous red-head with a pink petal mouth and adorable freckles on her pert little nose, but he had every intention sacrificing a chicken in gratitude. Which he would then bar-b-q, but he did not think that part would bear mentioning when he told the story later.

At the moment, his downed angel was attempting to wriggle her way off of him, which he was hampering because her firmly pinned back bun had become ensnared in one of the buttons of his coat. Chase knew that the gentlemanly thing to do was to call a truce to whatever wrestling match was currently taking place all over his front, but he was flat on his back and slightly out of air from taking a woman to the chest. And also, and probably most of importantly, he wasn't a gentleman and he really didn't want to stop any of the delightful shimmying that was taking place on top of him.

But there did seem to be a lot of distress, so he reached down and started pulling out bobby pins until everything came loose and the angel sat up. She perched on his stomach, skirt hitched up to her thighs, and blinked at him in apparent shock. He wasn't sure what gave her the right to be shocked—she was the one that had been flying through the air.

"I think I may have overshot," she said, breathlessly.

"That depends on what you were aiming for," he said. "If it was me, then you were right on target."

"I was attempting to reshelve *North American Piracy of the Nineteenth Century*," she said. She held up a book, still clutched in one hand.

"Well, what do you know," he said, looking at the worn cloth cover and gold embossed title. "That's a thing that exists. But yes, unless you were attempting to reshelve it in my sternum, then you vastly overshot."

The woman shaped missile flushed pink and struggled to stand up, pushing down her skirt as she went. If she was the librarian, then he was going to be checking out a lot of things that weren't books.

"I was just... I pushed too hard... the ladder..." She gestured toward the wall and he saw a sliding ladder contraption.

"You were playing Chutes and Ladders," he said, getting to his feet. "Got it."

"No!" She looked upset and attempted to swipe her hair back behind her ears, flushing pinker than ever. He wondered if she went pink everywhere when she blushed and how he could go about finding out. "I just got carried away," she said.

"Yes," he agreed. "And then you got carried into me."

She looked annoyed and opened her mouth as if to argue. He waited. Instead, she smoothed her skirt again and tried to stand up straighter. "Yes, fine. That is what happened. Can I help you with something? Why are you here? There aren't any tours today."

"Actually, I believe I'm looking for…" He pried the book out of her hand. "This. And anything else you have on a Spanish Galleon called the *San Buenaventura*."

One eyebrow went up and flustered was immediately replaced by sardonic. "Let me guess, you've got a great idea on where to find Regard's Treasure?"

"No," he said. "Haven't the foggiest. But I'm interested in finding out more about it."

Chase tried not to feel irritated as she sighed. He should have realized that everyone in Ashville would know about the treasure *and* have an opinion on it.

"The Spanish Galleon *San Buenaventura*," she said, her tone taking on an educational tone, as if she'd given this particular speech before, "purportedly loaded with king's ransom in gold and emeralds, was documented as having been sunk off the California coast by John Regard an Englishman who may or may not have been flying under the black flag at the time. From there he sailed up the coast and his ship was damaged in a storm. He anchored here, in the harbor of Ashville, and he left a month later when repairs were complete. But whether or not there was a treasure and whether or not he committed any crimes or acts of piracy while he was here… Those are all undocumented speculation. Feel free to pay the suggested fee and take the self-guiding tour."

"You seem very skeptical," he said.

"Everyone and his brother has hunted for that treasure.

Odds are, if it exists, it's in the water off of California. I don't deal in romantic myths here. If you want documented historical facts, there's a very well researched book by Thomas Ash from 1942 in the pirate section."

She pointed to some tall shelves by the window.

"That should be a laugh," said Chase. "Although, I suppose I do belong in the pirate section."

"What?" she frowned at him in puzzlement.

"Jenna!"

A lanky blond man strode into the library, interrupting Chase just as he was about to respond. Chase tried to decide if the man's argyle sweater was being worn ironically or if he just enjoyed looking like a Norman Rockwell painting.

"Did you do something different with you hair?" the man asked Jenna. "It looks nice."

Chase tried not to smile, now that he'd learned her name. Jenna had a nice ring to it.

Jenna avoided Chase's gaze and pushed another lock behind her ear. "Thanks," she muttered.

"Do we know each other?" asked the blond man frowning at Chase in disapproval. "You look familiar."

"Don't think so," said Chase, preparing to introduce himself. "I'm—"

"No time! This is urgent." Chase blinked at the preemptory tone as the man turned back to Jenna, literally turning his back on Chase. "The town council meeting is tonight, Jenna. You're going to be there, right?" Chase looked him up and down. He was tall and looked fit, but Chase thought he could take him. He needed knocked on ass just for his bad manners if nothing else.

Jenna sighed. "Will, honestly, don't you think you're making too much of this?"

"No! No, I'm not. That *thing* is a gaudy tourist trap. And it's historically inaccurate! It has bathrooms!"

"Well, I think we can all be grateful for that," said Jenna. Chase wasn't sure what Will was referring to, but he nodded his support for Jenna's opinion. He also drew the line on historical accuracy in bathrooms. No one in their right mind wanted a historically accurate bathroom.

"It was an affront to the good people of this town in 1818 and it's an affront now," said Will drawing himself up and lifting his chin in stentorian disapproval. Chase looked at Jenna to see what her response would be.

"I think it's delightful," said Jenna. "It's an amazing replica of Regard's *Revenge* and I think it brings life and vibrancy to our waterfront. We've had people from Portland and all over the state come to eat dinner on it and enjoy the show. I think it's fantastic to have a new business in town."

"It's not a business—it's carnival side show! Who wants sword fights over dinner? It's ridiculous!"

"So pirate ships are fine?" asked Chase, raising his eyebrows at Jenna. "But not pirate treasure?"

"It's not a pirate ship! It's a restaurant that happens to be pirate themed and located on a tall ship replica."

"It's a pirate ship," said Will and Chase at the same time.

"Oh, good grief," she said, throwing up her hands in exasperation.

"Perhaps if that idiot owner hadn't named it after the real ship we could have a conversation," continued Will, glaring at Chase. "But he did. And it's historically inaccurate!"

"Well, you can't expect the health department to approve food preparation in the galley of a historically accurate three-masted frigate," said Chase reasonably.

"I imagine the EPA probably wouldn't be fond of the bilge system either," said Jenna.

"Quite true," said Chase. "Also, the guests probably don't want to see the ocean when they lift the toilet lid."

"It does have that fluke man feeling," said Jenna.

"What?" Will looked from Chase to Jenna and back.

"There was that episode of X-files," said Jenna. "With a fluke man that would suck people down into the toilet. My brother made me watch it. I couldn't go into a port-a-potty for years afterward."

"I don't recommend going into them now," said Chase and Jenna chuckled.

"Although," she said, turning to him with a thoughtful expression, "that does rather raise the question of whether or not they actually had toilet lids on ships in 1818. I'm going to have to look that up."

"I'll save you the trouble," said Chase. "They did. They were latching of course. You don't want to leave anything open to the sea."

"That makes sense," said Jenna and she smiled at him. Chase felt like she'd hit him in the chest all over again. Her smile was enough to knock a man sideways.

"The point is," growled Will, glaring at Chase. "That thing is a monstrosity and I am going to petition the council to review all of his permits. You'll be there, right?" Will looked hopefully at Jenna and Chase could see that Will was going to be a problem, because Jenna wilted in the face of his sad-eyed hopeful stare.

"Will, I really don't think there is anything wrong with the ship. Also, I was going to go out with Sam tonight."

Chase added Sam to the problem category.

"Sam will understand," said Will, with what Chase thought was a complete lack of evidence.

"She won't understand," said Jenna. "We've missed like three girls nights in a row. I need margaritas!"

Chase took Sam back off the list. Margaritas and girls nights were two of his favorite things.

"Jenna!" Will looked aghast. "This is important!" There were more puppy dog eyes.

"Will," said Jenna, with a sigh. "I don't know… Maybe I could stop in for a minute."

"Great," said Chase. "Then I'll see you there."

"What?" Jenna and Will looked at him in confusion.

"I did try to mention this earlier," said Chase, with a smile. "I'm Chase Regard. That ship is my perfectly legal monstrosity and I'll be damned if I let you, or anyone else, get rid of it without a fight."

LEARN MORE: WWW.BETHANYMAINES.COM

FREE E-BOOK!
Go to
www.bethanymaines.com/free-e-book/
to collect a free e-story.

Blue Jones just stole Jake Garner's dog. And his heart. But technically the French Bulldog, Jacques, belongs to Jake's ex-girlfriend. And soon Jake is being pressured to return the dog and Blue is being targeted by mysterious attackers. Can Jake find Blue and Jacques before her stalkers do? For Blue, Christmas has never been quite so dangerous. For Jake, Christmas has never been quite so Blue.

Bethany Maines is the award-winning author of action adventure and fantasy tales that focus on women who know when to apply lipstick and when to apply a foot to someone's hind end. When she's not traveling to exotic lands, or kicking some serious butt with her black belt in karate, she can be found chasing after her daughter, or glued to the computer working on her next novel.

Juel Lugo is a graphic designer by day, business owner by trade, and flamenco dancer by sheer passion. She often finds herself roped into Bethany's "brilliant ideas". Her contributions to the saga of Luckless Love include helping craft the story and conducting in-depth wine research (spoiler alert: wine is delicious). Now, she's contentedly back to her daily grind, crafting stellar marketing messages and SEO-rich text that make search-bots swoon.

Also by Bethany Maines

CARRIE MAE MYSTERIES
Bulletproof Mascara
Compact With The Devil
High-Caliber Concealer
Glossed Cause

SAN JUAN ISLANDS MYSTERIES
An Unseen Current
Against the Undertow
An Unfamiliar Sea
An Unfinished Storm

SHARK SANTOYO CRIME SERIES
Shark's Instinct
Shark's Bite
Shark's Hunt
Shark's Fin
Peregrine's Flight
Shark's Blood

THE DEVERAUX LEGACY
(Romantic Suspense)
The Second Shot
A PNWA Literary ContesttAward Winner
The Cinderella Secret
The Hardest Hit
The Fallen Man

STAND ALONE NOVELS & NOVELLAS
Eye Contact
Love & Treasure
Lock & Key
Blue Christmas
Oh Holy Night
Winter Wonderland

THE SUPERNATURALS
(Paranormal Romance)
Wild Waters
A Little Red **(3 Colors #1)**
A Deeper Blue **(3 Colors #2)**
A Brighter Yellow **(3 Colors #3)**
Maverick
Hudson **(Rejects Pack #1)**
Killian **(Rejects Pack #2)**
Alekos **(Rejects Pack #3)**

GALACTIC DREAMS
When Stars Take Flight **Vol. 1**
The Seventh Swan **Vol. 2**
A Book Excellence Award Winner
The Beast of Arsu **Vol. 3**